A SCANDAL
MADE IN LONDON

A SCANDAL
MADE IN LONDON

LUCY KING

MILLS & BOON

First published in Great Britain 2020
by Mills & Boon, an imprint of HarperCollins*Publishers*
1 London Bridge Street, London, SE1 9GF

Large Print edition 2020

© 2020 Lucy King

ISBN: 978-0-263-08925-7

MIX
Paper from
responsible sources
FSC™ C007454

This book is produced from independently certified FSC™ paper to ensure responsible forest management. For more information visit www.harpercollins.co.uk/green.

Printed and bound in Great Britain
by CPI Group (UK) Ltd, Croydon, CR0 4YY

For Flo,
for all the support and encouragement.

CHAPTER ONE

WHAT ON *EARTH*…?

From behind his desk, situated on the top floor of the forty-four-storey building that housed the Knox Group, Theo Knox stared at the web page that filled the screen of the iPad that his head of security had just brought in and placed in front of him.

It appeared to be a table of information.

Harmony was the heading; below that came the details.

Geographical location: London
Age: 26
Height: 6' 1"
Vital statistics: 38-28-38
Hair: blonde
Eyes: blue
Tattoos: one
Interests: travel, books, music
Sexual experience: none

And the website? Belle's Angels, according to the elaborate logo involving entwined vines that shimmered in the top right corner. *'Matches made in heaven'*, apparently.

Which was all well and good, but of what use was any of this to him? And why did Antonio Scarlatto, a valued employee he'd previously considered competent and level-headed, think it would be?

Theo had absolutely no interest in dating sites, or in any kind of dating at all, since the occasional one-night stand when the need arose suited him fine. And even if he did, he had no time for it. As owner and CEO of a company that spanned the globe, employed thousands and was worth billions, he had a multitude of issues clamouring for his attention, the principle one of which currently was figuring out how he was going to persuade the ridiculously sentimental owner of the business he badly wanted to sell it to him.

'Why are you wasting my time by showing me this?' Theo demanded, lifting his gaze from the screen and levelling it at the man standing on the other side of the desk, who was way out of line if he thought Theo needed Harmony in his life.

'It relates to a current member of your staff,' said Antonio, not batting an eyelid in response to the dark look and arctic tone that usually had people quaking in their boots. 'She's registered on the site and this is her page. She tried to log in from her work computer twenty minutes ago. Our firewall flagged it up. As it's against company policy to access sites like this, I need to know what action to take.'

'It's a dating site,' Theo said flatly.

'It's not just a dating site,' Antonio countered. 'I wouldn't have disturbed you if it was. Scroll down.'

Mentally having to concede that point, Theo shoved a lid on his exasperation and switched his attention back to the tablet. He briefly ran his gaze over the table again, automatically registering and dismissing the information, then swiped up.

And froze.

Because to accompany Harmony's description were half a dozen photos. Of the woman in question in various outfits in various eye-popping poses. In the first four pictures, she was at least wearing clothes—short and tight and pretty revealing, but clothes nevertheless. In the last two, however, she wasn't wearing very much at all. Technically she had on a negligee, he saw, but she might as well not have bothered. It was so diaphanous it hid nothing that wasn't concealed under a few scraps of strategically placed lace beneath. Not her curves. Not the length of her limbs. Nothing.

And her face…

He knew that face.

It was Kate Cassidy.

Harmony, with her luscious body and dazzlingly striking looks, was Kate Cassidy.

The realisation hit Theo like a blow to the gut and he reeled.

What the hell was she up to?

Steeling himself, he scrolled down and read the text that accompanied the photos, and his blood turned to ice. Antonio had been right. Belle's Angels wasn't just any dating site and Kate wasn't after any kind of normal date *at all*.

As the implications of what he'd read and seen sank in, questions ricocheted around his head. What on earth was she thinking? Did she have *any* idea of the danger she could be putting herself in? More importantly, now he knew what she had planned, what was he going to do about it?

Because he'd definitely be doing *something*, he thought grimly as he clicked around the site, his horror growing with every passing second. Kate clearly needed looking out for. In fact, he should have been keeping an eye on her and her younger sister ever since their older brother Mike's death nine months ago. Discreetly. From afar. But nonetheless making sure they were as okay as they could be, because the debt he owed him was huge, because Mike had died because of something *he* could have prevented, and finally because they had no one else.

So why *hadn't* he done anything? Why hadn't he even been aware Kate was working for him? Guilt? Denial? The fact that these days he only seemed to function through sheer force of will?

Well, whatever it was, it stopped now because she, at least, was not okay. She'd evidently lost her tiny little mind. Furthermore, by signing herself up to this particular website she'd put herself at considerable risk, and that was unacceptable. The potential consequences didn't bear thinking about, and a person hurt—or worse—because he hadn't done enough to stop it simply could not happen again. Twice in one lifetime was more than enough.

'What action do you want me to take?' asked Antonio, cutting off Theo's thoughts before they could scythe through the fog of Mike's death and hurtle down memory lane to his own turbulent teenage years.

'Shut the site down,' Theo said as he pushed the tablet in Antonio's direction and slammed a mental door on Harmony's bio and the photos. 'Whatever it takes, however much it costs, shut it down.'

The head of security acknowledged the order with a brief nod of his head. 'And with regards to the employee in question?'

'I'll deal with her.'

Not once in the five and a half months she'd been working at the Knox Group had Kate been summoned to the hallowed top floor of the central London building that housed it, and that was fine with her. Her position as a middle-ranking accountant didn't merit the dubious honour, and, quite frankly, the less she had to do with the horrible Theo Knox, the better.

Not that they knew each other well, thank God. He might have been supposed 'friends' with her brother—although she struggled with the concept that her uptight, aloof *über* boss could ever do anything as human as *friends*—but she'd only met him once. At Mike's funeral nine months ago, in fact. And since that had hardly been a cordial encounter, she hadn't expected him to be in touch.

He was the man, after all, who'd coldly told her he wasn't interested and then turned his back on her when she'd made the monumental mistake of asking him for his support. All she'd wanted was a quick drink after the wake. To talk. Nothing more. Everyone else had left and she'd been distraught, feeling so horribly alone she'd simply wanted to prolong the afternoon by talking about her brother with someone who presumably had known him well. High and mighty Theo Knox, however, had evidently interpreted her suggestion as an invitation, and had treated it with the disdain and contempt he obviously felt it deserved before spinning on his heel and stalking off.

Kate had stood there staring at his retreating figure, open-mouthed and dumbstruck, unsure whether to laugh or cry because had he *really* thought she was coming on to him? At her brother's *funeral*? How inappropriate, how downright absurd, *was* that? His arrogance had been breathtaking. She'd never encountered self-absorption like it. Even worse was the lousy way his unwarranted rejection had made her feel. She shouldn't have cared what he thought of her since he meant absolutely nothing to her, yet his response had pulverised what little self-esteem she had, and for one blazing moment she'd never hated anyone more.

So if she'd been in any position to turn down the offer of a job at his company that had come her way shortly after, she'd have done so. However, she had bills to pay and the salary she'd been offered had been too generous to refuse. Not generous enough, of course, to cover the stratospheric sums of money her sister's residential care facility required, nor the repayment of the ever-increasing debt her brother had accrued to cover it, but definitely generous enough to make her want to pass her probationary period. And that was why, when she'd received the call from Theo's assistant requesting her presence on the top floor at precisely six p.m., the time she should have been leaving for home, she'd obeyed instead of telling him where to stick his imperious demand.

The lift she was travelling in slowed until it came to a smooth stop, and the doors opened with a soft swoosh. Automatically reminding herself not to slouch, Kate lifted her chin and crossed the plush white carpet that covered the floor with a long-legged stride.

When she arrived at the reception desk, she was waved in the direction of a pair of vast wooden doors, and headed towards them. Taking a deep breath, she knocked, and didn't have to wait long before a deep masculine voice barked, 'Come in.'

Kate braced herself and did as he'd commanded. The minute she walked through the door her attention instantly zoomed in on the man sitting behind the oak monolith of a desk, the man who was looking at her with a dark intensity and a stillness that radiated powerful authority and suggested complete and utter control.

Of her surroundings—the sleek white office so vast her entire flat would fit in it, the crystal-clear wall-to-wall windows that allowed the early evening late spring sunshine to flood in, the luxurious furnishings and the colourful pops of modern art on the walls—she was only dimly aware. All she was conscious of was her boss, the rude, condescending, hurtful jerk, and the memory of the intense loathing he'd once aroused in her.

'Shut the door.'

She did so, then walked towards him, the office becoming increasingly hot and claustrophobic with every step she took. Which, given the state-of-the-art temperature control the building had, was odd, and not a little disturbing.

As was the automatic way in which she seemed to be taking a mental inventory of his looks. At Mike's funeral she'd been in too great a state to register much about any of the guests, least of all him. Now, though, she had to grudgingly admit that the gossip columns, which lauded his appearance as much as they lamented his enigmatic elusiveness, were right. With his short dark hair, obsidian eyes and chiselled features he was easily the best-looking man she'd ever seen. The shoulders beneath the suit were impressively broad and they were matched by an equally impressive height, which she knew to be true because even though he was now sitting down, she'd just had a brief flash of memory of how she'd been in the unusual position of having to look up at him when she'd suggested a drink that afternoon.

He was also immaculate, she thought resentfully, taking in the perfection of his appearance as she advanced. Did he *ever* shove his hands through his hair in frustration? Ever permit even the *hint* of a five o'clock shadow? She doubted it. And had he ever been paralysed by self-doubt or plagued by rock-bottom self-esteem as she continually was? Even more unlikely. The man was a machine. A high-performing, single-minded, ruthlessly brilliant one, if the business press was to be believed, but a machine nevertheless.

Well.

Whatever.

What he was and how he looked were immaterial. So he was staggeringly handsome, in enviable control of himself and a good three or four inches taller than her. He was still a deeply unpleasant human being.

Coming to a halt a foot from the desk, Kate pulled herself together and reminded herself to stay calm, since it wouldn't do to reveal either how little she thought of him or how vulnerable she could be if she kept remembering how wretched he'd once made her feel. 'Mr Knox,' she said coolly. 'You wanted to see me?'

Something flickered in the depths of his dark eyes, something that flashed and burned and swiftly disappeared but nevertheless made her pulse skip a beat and her blood heat. 'I did,' he said with a brief nod in the direction of the two modern armchairs on her side of the desk. 'Theo will do. Sit down.'

'Thank you.'

Deliberately taking her time, Kate folded her six-foot-one frame into a chair and then spent a couple of vital seconds tugging her jacket down and smoothing her skirt. She needed to settle herself. This pulse-skipping, blood-heating business was ridiculous, as was the strange restlessness that churned around inside her. Nerves, most probably, because she had no idea why she'd been summoned and despite what she thought of him he *was* a bit intimidating. Or dread perhaps, the kind that came from knowing that one false move and the many plates she had spinning would crash to the ground. But still, either way, it was absurd.

'How are you?'

She stilled for a second and fought back a frown. What? *Now* he wanted pleasantries? Well, okay, she could do that. She could forget how they'd met for now. She couldn't imagine *he* remembered in any case. He certainly didn't appear to recognise her. 'Fine,' she said brightly, as if she weren't wrung out with stress and exhaustion. 'You?'

'Fine. Coffee?'

She gave her head a quick shake. 'No, thank you.'

'Tea?'

'No.'

'Anything?'

'I'm fine.'

'How's the job going?'

Hah. Which one? As well as being an accountant, she now worked in a bar five nights a week and dog-walked at the weekend. What little time she had left when she wasn't visiting her sister, she dedicated to the freelance bookkeeping work she'd also started to take on. 'Extremely well,' she said with a beaming smile, determined not to think about how close she was to the edge or how terrifying that was. 'I'm enjoying it very much.'

'Good,' he said, leaning forwards in a way that for some bizarre reason made her breath catch and her pulse skip a beat all over again. 'So. Kate. Tell me about Belle's Angels.'

And just like that—*bang!*—there went her composure. Talk about being lulled into a false sense of security, she thought, her smile fading as the churning started up again in her stomach. What did Theo Knox know about Belle's Angels? And how? Surely he couldn't be a member. He'd have no trouble getting a date. But had he visited the site? Had he seen her page? She had no idea why when her profile had racked up over a thousand views since she'd rashly stuck it up last night but the thought of *him* looking at her photos made her feel quite weak.

'What about it?' she said carefully, since his expression was giving absolutely nothing away.

'You're on it.'

Ah. Right. Busted.

Since Mr Knox—*Theo*—was allegedly insanely sharp, Kate didn't see the point in trying to come up with an excuse. 'I am,' she said, reminding herself that she had nothing to apologise for and nothing to be embarrassed about. What did it matter if he *had* seen her page? The photos were good. Empowering. Or something like that. At least she'd come up with a solution to the traumatic situation that had been robbing her of what little sleep she did get, even if it *had* had unexpected and rather unsettling consequences.

'You tried to access it while at work.'

Indeed she had. Earlier this afternoon. Her profile had attracted a great deal of interest, her alluded-to virginity in particular, and she'd been inundated with emails, some merely curious, some a bit odd, some downright creepy. Not having a clue what to do about any of it and wanting the deluge to stop, she'd decided to alter her account settings while she figured it out. 'I did.'

'Which is an infringement of company policy.'

At that Kate went very still, her heart giving a great lurch.

Oh.

Oh, dear.

That hadn't occurred to her. But it should have done because of *course* it would be. Belle's Angels, registered in Germany and possibly skirting the boundaries of legality in the UK, was just the sort of website that would be blocked by a firewall. Which was undoubtedly why it hadn't opened. She hadn't thought to reflect upon that. She'd just wanted to switch off the interminable stream of responses. But clearly she'd been an idiot. More than an idiot, actually. She could very well have put herself out of a job.

'That was a mistake,' she said as the potential ramifications raced through her head and a sweat broke out all over her skin. 'A one-off. It won't happen again.'

'You're right,' he said flatly, his eyes dark and inscrutable. 'It won't.'

A ball lodged in her throat and she swallowed it down with difficulty. 'Are you firing me?' she asked, the rising panic making her voice tight.

She needed this job, she needed *all* her jobs, but if she lost *this* one, she'd be in even more serious trouble than she already was. Fired accountants weren't exactly desirable potential employees and who knew how long it would be before she got another job? The bills were mounting up daily and the correspondence from the debt agency was growing increasingly threatening, not that her salary was anywhere *near* enough to cover the repayments or the cost of her sister's care, but Milly depended on her and *only* her since there was no one else now Mike had died, and if she had to leave Fairview she'd be devastated, and, oh, she *really* should have thought this whole crazy plan through.

'I'm not firing you.'

Phew.

'Then what do you mean?' she said as her racing heart slowed and the jumble of panicky thoughts faded.

'I had the site shut down.'

What? The tension that had ebbed a moment ago shot straight back.

No.

No.

This was *not* good.

'You can't do that,' she breathed, appalled, as it dawned on her that if what Theo was saying was true then he'd scuppered what, as far as she could see, was her only chance of making some serious, much-needed money fast.

'I can,' he said grimly. 'And I have.'

'How?'

'It wasn't hard.'

No, it wouldn't be to a man of his considerable influence and power, but— 'You had no right.'

'Probably not.'

'So why?'

His eyebrows shot up, the only sign of expression she'd seen in him since she'd walked in. *'Why?'*

'Yes, why?' What was it to him? Even if he *did* know who she was, which was doubtful, why would he care all of a sudden?

'You signed up to an escort agency, Kate.'

His tone was brutal and icily condemning but she refused to be intimidated. It was all very well for him and his billions in the bank. Lesser mortals had to think more creatively if they didn't want to firstly destroy the happiness and security of their vulnerable younger sister, secondly lose the home they'd once shared with their adored, much-missed brother and lastly be declared bankrupt and never work in the field they loved again.

'And so what?' she said, resisting the urge to lift her chin since a punchy show of defiance could well make him reassess his decision not to fire her.

'How could you be so reckless?'

Reckless? She wasn't reckless. Desperate and exhausted and all out of options, yes, but reckless, no. 'I'm not. I did my research.'

'So did I,' he said ominously.

'Well, then.'

'Belle's Angels is basically an online brothel.'

'Possibly,' she had to admit, since there *was* that aspect to it, 'but it's a very high-class one.'

A tiny muscle began to tic in his jaw. 'That is utterly irrelevant.'

'No,' she said. 'It isn't. Because *this* one has different levels of service agreement, and I only signed up to level one.'

He looked at her as if she'd grown two heads. 'Did you honestly think someone was going to pay you a thousand pounds an hour for *conversation*?'

'Why not?' she said. 'My conversational skills are first class.'

'I have no doubt they are. However, believe me, your...*clients*...would have been expecting far more.'

'Yes, well, you obviously have more experience of such sites than I do.'

In response to her demure yet pointed little dig Theo's face darkened and the look he gave her was hard and forbidding. 'I've heard stories,' he said flatly. 'None of them good. Do you have *any* idea of how dangerous it could have been?'

Kate opened her mouth to reply and then closed it because he might have a point there. Truth be told, she hadn't exactly been thinking entirely rationally when she'd signed up to the site late last night. Another exorbitant bill had just come through from Fairview on top of a none-too-friendly email from the loan company Mike had used *and* a letter from her mortgage company informing her that she'd missed a payment, as if she needed reminding.

She'd had a couple of glasses of wine to dull the resulting anxiety, but they hadn't worked; they'd just made her feel even sicker. A documentary about webcamming had been on TV in the background, and in the midst of her despair it had suddenly struck her that sex sold. Extremely well, apparently. And while she wasn't desperate enough—yet—to perform for the camera, she'd figured there had to be other less extreme options.

It had been remarkably easy to find an appropriate site and register. When she remembered the stash of normal-sized clothes she'd bought over the years because it made her feel dainty and feminine just to know she owned them even though none of them actually fitted, it had seemed as though the stars had aligned. In fact, the most challenging aspect of the whole exercise had been mastering the self-timer on her phone.

Of course she'd considered the possible consequences of her plan—she wasn't a *complete* fool—but she'd been at her wits' end and as a result her assessment had been brief. Conveniently, the pros had vastly outweighed the cons. What cons there were—mainly concerning the sort of people who might use such a site—she'd presumed would be neutralised by the application of filters and a robust screening process.

Clearly, however, there'd been little of that because some of the creepier emails she'd received had been downright disturbing. The staggering sums of money she'd been offered for her virginity, not to mention the many ways it could apparently be relieved, had been even more alarming. And, actually, even the more moderate correspondence had hinted at something other than conversation, so maybe Theo also had a point about her would-be clients' expectations.

Perhaps, then, in hindsight, she'd had a lucky escape, even if it did mean that her only hope had vanished and she was now back at a terrifying square one. Because if she was being brutally honest, the reality of what the site offered was far seedier than in her naivety she'd imagined, and, regardless of the amount of money on offer, the thought of actually having to go through with some of the more lurid scenarios described made her want to throw up.

'It is absolutely *none* of your business,' she said, not inclined to admit that Theo could be right and give him the upper hand.

'That's not strictly true.'

No. Well. There was the small issue of pesky company policy, but still. He had no right to meddle in her affairs in this way. In *any* way. 'I don't need rescuing, Theo,' she said steadily. 'I'm twenty-six. I'm eminently sensible and perfectly capable of making my own choices.' Not that she had many at this precise moment.

'It doesn't look like it from where I'm sitting.'

Ooh, he was insufferable. 'Why do you even *care*?'

He stared at her silently for a moment, as if he couldn't work it out either, and the hard intensity of his gaze coupled with the way he seemed to be trying to see into her soul was sending a strange sluggish heat oozing through her blood, detonating tiny sparks along her veins and electrifying her nerves.

To her consternation she found she couldn't look away. She could hardly breathe. All of a sudden she wanted to get up, clamber over his desk and plaster herself against him. And then she wanted to—well, she wasn't quite sure what she wanted to do next since she had little experience of such things, but she wanted to find out. So badly she was ablaze with it.

Appalled at and bewildered by her reaction, she shifted in an attempt to alleviate the fizzing of her stomach and the prickling of her heated skin, but all that did was inch her skirt up her thighs, at which point Theo's darkening gaze dropped to her legs and lingered there a while, which sent the heat buzzing through her shooting straight down to the spot where she suddenly, *alarmingly*, burned.

Maybe she moved again, maybe she let out an audibly breathy gasp. She didn't know. But Theo jerked his gaze back up, his expression once again cold and inscrutable, and the tension snapped.

'I take it you need the money,' he said bluntly, and all she could think was money? What money?

Ah.

Well, of course she needed the money, she thought, tugging her skirt back down with annoyingly shaky fingers as the reminder of her precarious financial state obliterated the bizarre heat and dizziness and refocused her attention. Why else would she do it? She wasn't *that* desperate for a date. 'I do.'

'How much?'

'A lump sum of a hundred thousand, plus around five thousand a month on an on-going basis for the next sixty, possibly seventy, years.'

Up shot his eyebrows. 'That's a lot of money.' *Really?*

'I am aware of that,' she said coolly. And now, thanks to him and his high-handed ways, it was a lot of money she still had to somehow find because, quite apart from the distressing threat of homelessness, she was *not* having Milly moved when she was so happy and secure where she was.

'It's a concern,' he said.

'You're telling me.'

'It's *my* concern.'

'How?'

'You're an accountant,' he said. 'You're about to finish your probation, at which point you will have access to certain aspects of the company's bank accounts. Fraud is a risk.'

What the—?

Kate blinked at him, for a moment completely lost for words. Was he being serious? 'Are you suggesting I might indulge in a little light embezzlement in order to pay my bills?'

'It's a possibility.'

'It is *not* a possibility because I am *not* a criminal,' she said heatedly.

'What do you need it for?'

Kate took a deep breath to soothe the outrage surging through her. 'I have a younger sister,' she said. 'Milly. She was in the car accident that killed our parents ten years ago.' She swallowed hard but made herself continue. 'She survived but she suffered catastrophic brain injuries. She can't live on her own. She needs twenty-four-hour care. The insurance pay-out only covers the most basic of facilities, which just aren't good enough.'

For a few long moments, Theo said nothing, just frowned. And then he nodded, as if something in his head had slotted into place. 'Your brother used to fund the rest.'

Ah. So he *did* know who she was.

Well.

'He did,' she said, steeling herself against the surge of grief that still sometimes shot out of nowhere and walloped her in the chest. 'And there was some money from his estate, but it's run out.'

'His flat?'

'Rented. A few months before his death he gave it up and moved in with me.'

'Life insurance?'

'He didn't have any.' If only. 'Believe me, if there was any money anywhere I'd have found it. After he died I discovered that he'd been taking out high-interest loans. They need repaying, like, yesterday.'

'I see.'

Did he? she wondered, swallowing down the tight ball of emotion that had lodged in her throat. She doubted it. The gut-wrenching combination of despair, guilt, anger, grief and dread she'd felt when she'd found out what Mike had done had to be unique. Besides, had Theo ever needed money so badly he'd do anything to get it? Unlikely. He'd made his first million by the age of seventeen and his fortune had rocketed year on year since.

'You'll have it.'

She stared at him in bewilderment. What was

he talking about? Have it? Have what? 'I'm sorry?'

'Give me the details and I'll pay off the debt and set up a trust fund to pay for whatever your sister needs for however long she needs it.'

What?

Oh.

Right.

Wow.

'Are you serious?' she asked in stunned disbelief.

'Yes.'

'Why would you do that?'

His eyes clouded and she caught a glimpse of what bizarrely looked like...what? Guilt? Anguish? Regret? As if. By all accounts he didn't do emotion any more than he did friends, so who knew? It was most likely irritation that he'd had to interrupt his no doubt busy schedule to deal with what he perceived to be a problem. 'Because I can,' he said eventually.

That was undeniably true. He was one of the ten richest men in the world according to one newspaper article she'd read. What she needed might amount to millions but to him it was a rounding error. Nevertheless, what ultra-successful reportedly ruthless businessman did something like that?

'Do you really expect me to believe you're that altruistic?' she asked, unable to keep the scepticism from her tone.

'I don't particularly care what you believe.'

Nice. 'Well, thank you,' she said primly. 'But I can't accept it.'

'Why not?'

Hmm. Where to start? Because she didn't like him and the thought of being indebted to a man she loathed was abhorrent? Because any man who could single-handedly close down a large, foreign website was to be treated with caution and she didn't trust him an inch? She could hardly tell him any of that. He was still her boss.

'It's too much,' she said instead.

'Not from my perspective.'

'Still no.'

'Where else are you going to get the money?'

'I'll think of something.' Hadn't her brief foray into the shady world of online escorts proved that? Surely she'd be able to come up with a workable solution, one that didn't involve seedy sex or overbearing men.

'It sounds like you'd better think of it quickly.'

Well, yes, there was that. She was running out

of time. Fast. How much longer did she have? How much more could she take? She was *so* tired of worrying about the money. About the debt and the reduced quality of life her sister might have if she had to move because she—Kate—had failed. About losing her home and the precious memories she had of her brother. The responsibilities she now had, which landed entirely on her shoulders, were crushing, bewildering, overwhelming. Sometimes she wished she could just go to bed for a month and cry.

'Just out of interest, what would you want in return?' she asked, because even if she had been considering it, which she wasn't, surely that amount of money would come with strings.

'Nothing.'

She stared at him. 'Nothing?'

He gave a brief nod. 'That's right.'

'Why not?'

'Do I need a reason?'

'*I* would. You're in the business of deal-making. No one ever gets something for nothing. Even I know that.'

'You have my word.'

'I don't know what your word is worth.' What if hypothetically she agreed and he suddenly decided that his money gave him the right to influence Milly's future? What if at some point he decided to stop?

'I'll have a contract drawn up,' he said, clearly able to read the scepticism that must have been written all over her face. 'You can state the terms. I won't challenge them.'

'Things that sound too good to be true generally are.'

His jaw tightened. 'Just accept my offer, Kate. It's the only one on the table.'

True. But— 'I'd never be able to repay you.'

'There'd be no need.'

'I'd feel a need.'

'Then I suggest you get over it,' he said tersely, 'because you should know that I will be doing this, with or without your consent. Your agreement will merely speed things up.'

And quite suddenly, in the face of such intransigence, what remained of Kate's resistance suddenly crumbled. Why was she still fighting this? She was running on fumes and at her wits' end. What Theo was proposing would obliterate all her worries and stresses overnight. So if he could afford it and wanted to help, why shouldn't she let him? Maybe he *did* feel something after all. Maybe he and Mike *had* been good friends. Ultimately, did it even matter? She didn't need to like him, and his motivations were none of her concern. He was offering her a 'no strings attached' deal, which would get the debt collectors off her back and, more importantly, ensure Milly's comfort for the rest of her life as well as the best treatments available. So despite feeling as though she might be making a deal with the devil, she couldn't *not* accept his help. She just couldn't.

'Okay, fine,' she said with a brief nod. 'You win.'

CHAPTER TWO

He'd won, had he?

Hmm…

Theo wasn't so sure. He might have achieved the outcome he'd been intent on getting, but in reality, given the massive debt he owed Mike, the provision of financial support for Kate and her sister was long overdue and it certainly didn't lessen the crushing omnipresent guilt he felt over the part he'd played in their brother's death. If anything, it made it worse because he hadn't known about the loans and he should have.

And then there was the battle for his self-control, which he'd started waging the moment Kate had walked into his office and detonated a savagely fierce and wholly unexpected reaction inside him. Was he winning that? By the skin of his teeth, and only then because he had years of practice.

He had not been prepared for her effect on him. The first and last time they'd met—at her brother's funeral, an insanely tough and gruelling experience for a number of reasons—had certainly given no indication. This evening, however, she'd come through that door and for some unfathomable reason every sense he possessed had instantly sprung to high alert. The way she'd moved—languidly and sinuously graceful—had mesmerised him, and as she'd approached his desk, that web page she'd set up had slammed back into his head. So much for thinking he'd successfully excised it from his memory. Clearly he'd merely drawn a veil across it, a veil that her appearance in his space had instantly swept back.

With every step she took towards him, his blood had begun to heat and questions had started ricocheting around his head. Forget her vital statistics and her hobbies, he'd thought, his pulse thudding heavily and his body hardening. What he'd like to know more about was the tattoo. Where was it, and what was it of?

Then there was the tiny yet somehow momentous detail regarding her sexual experience. The 'none' of it implied that she was still a virgin, but regardless of its meaning, it shouldn't have been of the slightest interest. However, infuriatingly, he seemed to find it fascinating because all he could think was, why? She was twenty-six and it couldn't be from lack of opportunity. She looked like a goddess. Not, perhaps, conventionally beautiful, but certainly breathtakingly striking with her long blonde hair and big blue eyes and above average height.

And last, but by no means least, there were the photos, the last two in particular, which once seen could not unfortunately be unseen and were now indelibly etched into his memory. Those had had him instinctively thinking about the suite adjoining his office, the oversized bed he had in there, and her sprawled across it wearing nothing but that negligee.

Such a savage and unexpected assault on his senses had decimated his self-control and his body had responded—and was still responding—in the inevitable way, hence the subsequent battle.

However, he was concealing the attraction scorching through his blood effectively enough and he was well used to conducting a conversation that bore no reality to what was going on inside him. He might have been momentarily distracted when she'd shifted and the movement had exposed even more lovely long leg that he'd suddenly, *appallingly*, wanted to touch, but their discussion had remained—and would continue to remain—firmly on track. Kate would never have any idea of the fierce need pounding away inside him. It was purely physical and of zero importance anyway, and nothing she could do or say would ever entice him to yield to it. Not the blush on her cheeks, not the darkening of her irises, not the soft breathy gasp.

'Is there anything else you need?' he said coolly, his voice bearing not even a hint of the inner turmoil he was experiencing.

'No. Thank you. I have everything else under control.'

Lucky her. 'Let me know if that changes.'

'Of course,' she said, about to move again before clearly thinking the better of it, thank *God*, and adding, 'And, actually, thank you for your offer of help. That "you win" of mine was churlish.'

'It was.'

'Although, to be fair, you *had* just ridden roughshod over my plans without any consideration for my feelings.'

She had a point, just not one he could bring himself to apologise for. 'Perhaps.'

'Nevertheless, that's no excuse,' she continued. 'I apologise. My parents were particularly hot on manners. They'd be spinning in their graves at my lack of them…' She tailed off for a moment, a flash of sorrow flitting across her expression, but then gave herself a quick shake. 'Anyway,' she said briskly, 'I really am grateful for your offer. And since this seems to be the moment for it, I suppose I also ought to thank you for closing down that website.'

Sitting back and ignoring the desire to respond to that moment of grief because he didn't do emotion and it was no business of his anyway, Theo rested his elbows on the arms of his chair. 'Oh?' he said, arching an eyebrow since only five minutes ago she'd been outraged by what he'd done. 'Why?'

'There were emails,' she said with a shudder. 'Disturbing ones. There are some very sick people out there.'

'What did you expect?' he said, not even wanting to *think* about the offers she might have received.

'I'm not entirely sure,' she said with a naivety he envied because he'd give everything he had not to know the depths people could sink to. 'A few emails perhaps, maybe resulting in one or two regular clients with more money than sense. Certainly not *that* kind of a response. To be honest, it never occurred to me that my virginity would cause such a furore.'

He'd never have imagined taking such an interest in it either. He still couldn't work out why he did. 'You are pretty unique.'

Her eyebrows lifted and another blush tinged her cheeks. 'Am I?'

'In this day and age a twenty-six-year-old virgin is unusual.'

She appeared to deflate for a moment, but then rallied. 'I suppose so,' she said with a shrug.

'What's the issue?'

'It's none of your business.'

'True.'

She tilted her head. 'Why would you want to know anyway?'

Good question. He barely knew her. He didn't do personal and didn't need to know. He certainly had no intention of helping her out with it, and where the hell had that idea even *come* from? Nonetheless, he could tell himself all he liked that it was important to be in full possession of all the facts so he could stop her embarking on any further acts of recklessness, but the plain truth was that for some reason he just wanted to know. 'I'm curious.'

'It's hardly an appropriate topic for a boss/employee conversation,' she countered. 'And besides, I'm still on probation.'

No problem there. He'd spoken to her line manager in the accounts department earlier just in case she did need firing. Fortunately, she didn't. Her work was superb and she was a reliable, valued member of the team.

'You're excellent at your job,' he said. 'You'll pass it. And we crossed the boss/employee line the minute you tried to access the Belle's Angels site from a computer I own.'

'Nevertheless, no.'

'Okay, fine,' he said, annoyed with himself for pushing it. He wasn't *that* curious, dammit. If she didn't want to tell him, so what? In fact, it was a good thing, because she ought to go. The battle he was having to keep his eyes off her legs and his mind off the rest of her was taking more effort than he'd anticipated. Their business was concluded and, frankly, the sooner he could get back to work, back to *normal*, the better. 'You can see yourself out.'

Kate watched Theo nod in the direction of the door and then turn his attention to whatever was on his computer screen, and thought that if that wasn't a cue to leave, she didn't know what was. As dismissals went it was unambiguous. She'd refused to play ball and he'd lost interest. Which was fine. There was no way she was going to share the issues surrounding her non-existent sex-life with her boss, of all people. Imagine the humiliation. It didn't bear thinking about.

Therefore his cue was one she was going to take. Right now. She was going to get up, waltz out and go home, where she could ponder at length this evening's whole surreal conversation and, when it came to her money troubles, pinch herself hard.

So why wasn't she moving? Why did her bottom appear to be glued to the chair? Why was her heart hammering at such a rate it might crack a rib and why was a cold sweat breaking out all over her skin? She couldn't actually be thinking of telling him what he wanted to know, could she?

No. It was out of the question. Theo Knox was the very *last* man she ought to want to confide in, although her brother had obviously had time for the guy and he *was* prepared to come through for Milly so maybe he wasn't all bad. But that was irrelevant. Spilling her innermost thoughts and fears to him would be insane. Complete and utter professional suicide. Not to mention epically mortifying. Besides, why would she even *want* to? She shouldn't. She *didn't*.

And yet, to her horror, it was growing increasingly tempting to think to hell with it and throw caution to the wind. She could feel the pressure to do exactly that building unbearably inside her, and the words were on the tip of her tongue, piling up one on top of the other, clamouring for release.

What was going on? she wondered in mounting panic, clamping her lips together as horror thundered through her. Had the stress of everything that had happened lately finally broken her down? Had Theo cunningly deployed some sort of reverse psychology that suddenly had her desperate to share every tiny detail? Or was it simply that now she'd experienced a smidgeon of his interest she wanted more?

Impossible, she told herself as she took a deep breath through her nose and willed the dizziness to subside. That would be utterly ridiculous. She wasn't that pathetic. She certainly wasn't so starved of attention that she'd forfeit her dignity and fall on any crumb dropped at her feet.

But when *was* the last time a man had expressed any interest in her? Ever? Okay, so Theo had made it perfectly clear at Mike's funeral he wasn't interested in her like *that*, and that was fine because it wasn't as if she wanted him to do anything about her little problem, was it? Heaven forbid. When she did finally get around to losing her virginity she didn't want him anywhere near her. He was rude, high-handed and unpleasant and made her bristle with loathing, although, come to think of it, it wasn't loathing she'd been bristling with for the last quarter of an hour. She wasn't entirely sure what it was, any more than she understood what that charged moment when he'd looked at her legs had been about. The blessed relief that her money worries were over, most probably.

It couldn't be anything else. It certainly couldn't be attraction. What a waste of time and energy *that* would be. Even if she *had* liked him, Theo Knox was so far out of her league he was on another planet. He was a staggeringly handsome, enormously successful billionaire. She was an inexperienced ordinary woman of significantly above average height, who managed to look passable on a good day in the right clothes, of which, truth be told, she had few since it was expensive to clothe well a body like hers. She was moderately good at her job and reasonably intelligent, but she wasn't beautiful. She wasn't special. In fact, she was the very opposite of special.

But regardless of her non-specialness, *something* about what she'd done had caught his attention enough to summon her up here and grill her when he could have just had her fired. And that was more appealing than it ought to be.

And so it seemed that—oh, dear—she *was* that pitiful and she *was* that starved of attention, because whatever the cost to her pride she wanted Theo's interest back. She wanted to matter to someone. It was undoubtedly stupid and she definitely didn't want to think about what it said about her, but the longer she sat there, the more inevitable it became, the more powerful was the urge to share, and she suddenly didn't have the strength to resist.

'Well, if you *really* want to know,' she said, vaguely wondering if she hadn't completely lost the plot, 'mainly it's my height.'

'What?' Theo snapped as he whipped his head round, his deep scowl clearly indicating his displeasure at her continued presence.

'It's my height.'

'What the hell does that have to do with anything?'

'Everything.'

'Why? Lying down—or in most other positions, for that matter—height makes absolutely no difference.'

What?

Okay...

'Well, naturally I don't know much about that,' she said, hoping she wasn't blushing quite as madly as she suspected and wishing she had stronger willpower. 'But I hit six foot some time around my fifteenth birthday. I was lanky and clumsy and towered over the boys in my class at school. When it came to adolescent hook-ups they gave me a wide berth. There were plenty of other more normal girls to choose from.'

'There is nothing abnormal about you,' he said darkly, his gaze roaming all over her and setting her skin on fire.

'Others might beg to differ,' she said, determinedly ignoring it. 'It was a difficult time anyway. My parents had just died and my twelve-year-old sister was in hospital, fighting for survival. Life as I knew it had shattered. Most people were kind and full of sympathy. Others, not so much. Some didn't know how to handle it, well, me, really, and teenagers can be cruel, can't they?'

His eyes narrowed. 'What did they do?'

'It was more a case of what they *said*,' she said,

her throat tightening as she recalled the grief, pain and confusion that had dominated her emotions during that time. 'There were a lot of stupid, nasty rumours going round. A few bitchy comments. On one particularly memorable occasion a boy came up to me and said that my parents must have deliberately crashed because death was preferable to the embarrassment of having such a freak for a daughter.'

There was a pause, during which Theo's jaw clenched imperceptibly and his entire body seemed to tense. 'I literally have no words,' he said eventually.

'No, well, that wasn't pleasant. It took me a while to get over it all, the loss of my parents, the new reality my sister faced, the bullying and then the guilt that my brother had been forced to leave university to come and look after me. And then when I did—which was no mean feat, I can tell you, not least because part of me was convinced that it wasn't fair of me to live my life when Milly's had been so devastatingly curtailed—it was to discover that even grown men are put off by my height. Apparently it's emasculating. Not to mention intimidating.'

A tiny muscle began to hammer in Theo's cheek. 'That's pathetic,' he said grimly.

'I know,' she said with a casual 'what can you do?' kind of shrug, as if the years of bullying and rejection that had crippled her self-esteem and destroyed her sense of self-worth meant nothing. 'But, well, it was what it was and on the upside, all that time my classmates and fellow uni students were dating I spent studying. I got a first-class degree and now have a career I love.'

'I find your height neither emasculating nor intimidating,' said Theo, his eyes not leaving hers for a second.

'Why would you?' she said as a tiny shiver raced down her spine. 'You're a hugely successful businessman with the world at his fingertips. I doubt you're intimidated by anything.' Or emasculated. He oozed such virile masculinity it simply wasn't possible.

'You'd be surprised.'

As his mouth curved into a faint smile, Kate thought that this was another of those occasions she wanted to look away. More than she wanted to know what intimidated him, which was saying something. The intensity of his gaze was making her skin feel all hot and prickly and yet again she was finding it oddly hard to breathe. She felt trapped. On fire. And suddenly, quite out of the blue, acutely aware of him.

Inexplicably, the tiniest of details began to register. The minute scar that bisected his right eyebrow. The slight bump on the bridge of his nose. And was that a silvery grey hair she could see at his left temple in amongst all the ebony? She rather thought it was.

And it wasn't only the physical details that she now noticed. She could sense the tension radiating off him and the power he was keeping tightly leashed. The non-verbal signals he was emanating gave her the impression he was furious. On her behalf. And although she had no idea why that would be the case it made her go all warm and fuzzy.

What would it have been like to have had someone like him on her side when she'd been at school? she couldn't help wondering as the silence stretching between them thickened. What would it feel like now?

Come to think of it, what would *he* feel like? He'd be hard and muscled, she was sure. All over. He wasn't the type to tolerate softness. Except maybe where his lips were concerned. Those looked nice and velvety. And what about the sprinkling of dark hair she could see on the backs of his hands? Would it be rough to the touch or silky? And where else might he have it?

She had no way of knowing, and now, bizarrely, that, as well as the realisation she'd never find out how soft his lips actually were, seemed a shame.

'Anyway,' she said, baffled by the unexpectedly carnal turn of her thoughts and suddenly really rather keen to lighten the weirdly tense atmosphere, 'your experience of height has probably been far different from mine.'

Theo started, as if she'd jerked him out of deep thought, and his brows snapped together. 'Has it?'

'Has anyone asked you what the weather's like up there?'

'No.'

'Suggested a career in basketball?'

'No.'

'I bet you haven't ever had to put up with tiny little aeroplane seats and bashed knees.'

'I have a private jet.'

Of course he did. 'I always wanted a little zippy convertible,' she said with a whimsical sigh. He nodded and she thought for a nanosecond that maybe he did understand after all. 'Being hugged is a problem.'

'Is it?'

'Yes,' she said with a nod, although it wouldn't

be a problem if it was Theo doing the hugging, would it? Her head would tuck into his neck perfectly. Her body would fit against his beautifully. And then she'd know exactly how hard and muscled he was...

'Doorways.'

What? Oh. 'Pendant lights.'

'Hotel showers.'

Not helping. But what was going on? Why was she so flustered by the thought of Theo in the shower? Why was she even *thinking* about Theo in the shower? And why did she get the impression he was thinking about her in the shower? Unanswerable questions all of them, so she put them out of her mind and focused. 'Much of the world is structurally tallist, don't you think?' she said, thankfully sounding more in control than she felt.

'It is,' he said with the glimmer of a smile so fleeting the minute it was gone she thought she must have imagined it.

'Sleeves?'

'My clothes are tailor-made.' Naturally. 'Shoes?'

'Nightmare,' she said. 'I'm a size nine. And I never wear heels. You?'

'Heels have never been my thing,' he said, that faint smile back again.

Kate nearly fell off her chair because, good heavens, was that a *joke*? Crikey.

'It's hard to be inconspicuous.'

He arched an eyebrow. 'Is that a negative?'

It was for her. She'd been taller than her contemporaries since the moment she'd learned to walk. Throughout her childhood barely a week had passed without someone commenting on it. She couldn't remember a time she hadn't felt different, and not in a good way. No amount of positive parental input had helped. She'd just wanted to be the same as everyone else. To fit in. Subsequently she'd spent so much of her childhood and teenage years hunching her shoulders and trying to appear shorter than she was her posture was abysmal. 'I imagine that depends who you are.'

'You command attention.'

Obviously he was using the 'you' in the general sense, not referring to her in particular, but nevertheless she weirdly found herself sitting up a bit straighter. 'Possibly,' she hedged.

'And statistically, taller people tend to earn a higher salary.'

Her eyebrows lifted. 'Really?' That *was* interesting.

'So I once read.'

'I must remember that at my next performance review.'

'I would.' He paused, then said, 'Light bulbs.'

'Maxi-dresses,' she batted back.

'You never have a problem reaching for something from a high shelf.'

'And you can always spot friends in a crowd.'

'Quite,' he said. 'Definite pluses.'

His words were spoken evenly enough, but something flickered across his expression and the smile faded, and it suddenly occurred to her that while she'd assumed he was too uptight and aloof to do friends, maybe it wasn't just that. Maybe it was more that it was lonely at the top. And so maybe he was as lonely as she was...

Or not.

The strangely electric heat surging through her dissipated and she went cold, because what planet was she *on*? A man like Theo would never be lonely. He certainly wouldn't lack for female companionship. Just because nothing appeared about him in the gossip columns didn't mean he was a monk. And a moment or two of banter did not make him a kindred spirit. She must have been mad to imagine he ever could be. And to think she'd even harboured the vague hope that he might have some advice for her about how to deal with an excess of centimetres. Of course he wouldn't. He clearly had no hang-ups about anything at all, and why would he? He was a god and she was about as far from goddess-ness as it was possible to get. She and Theo were poles apart in virtually every way. She had to be even more starved of attention than she realised if she was deluding herself with the idea that they somehow shared something unique. And as for the inappropriate little fantasies about hugging and showers, what had she been *thinking*?

The setting sun was casting an oddly seductive golden glow across his office and the sense of intimacy it created was messing with her head. That was the trouble. It spun a sort of web that rendered reality all blurry. That was why she found it so easy to talk to him. Why she'd been all of a flutter when he'd so casually mentioned the many sexual positions he'd obviously experienced.

The sooner she could get out of here, the better. If she stayed, who knew what else she might reveal? She'd already humiliated herself quite enough. Once she'd started talking she hadn't shut up. Besides, what with the rolling of her stomach and the bizarre way she kept going hot and cold at the same time, she was beginning to feel very peculiar indeed.

'So, anyway,' she said with a feebly bright smile. 'There you are. The reasons why I'm still a virgin. Basically no one wants me. And on that pretty mortifying note I should definitely go. I'm sure you have plenty to be getting on with and I've taken up more than enough of your time. So, sorry for the firewall breach thing and, uh, thanks for everything... I'd best be off. Unless, of course, there's anything else?'

CHAPTER THREE

ANYTHING ELSE?

Anything else?

God.

There was so much going on in Theo's head he didn't know how to even *begin* to unravel it. How he was managing to keep a grip on things he had no idea. If he'd known what chaos Kate was going to unleash by not leaving when he'd told her to, he'd have picked her up and carried her out instead of ignoring his better judgement and like an idiot encouraging her to continue.

When she'd been talking about everything she'd been through his entire body had started to churn. When she'd mentioned the short-sighted fools who'd rejected her over the years he'd had an irrational urge to demand a list of names. When she'd revealed that she'd been bullied and how, his hands had curled into fists and he'd wanted to hit something for the first time in fourteen years, six months and ten days. As they'd batted back and forth the pros and cons of being tall, for the briefest of moments he'd forgotten where and who he was and had found himself actually enjoying the conversation, until she'd mentioned friends and he'd crashed back down to earth with a bump.

And then there was the want, the searing, clawing, deeply inappropriate need to show her what the soft gasps and blushes meant and what her body was capable of. Of what they'd be capable of together, because when she'd looked him as if she was somehow imagining him naked he'd nearly combusted.

The strength of his reaction to this woman didn't make any sense. She was by no means the most beautiful woman he'd ever met and he'd always preferred sophisticated experience over naivety. He had absolutely no reason to behave and feel the way he did around her. It was too visceral, too dramatic, and wholly unacceptable.

Why did he even care about her issues anyway? And why had he taken such umbrage to her registration to that site in the first place? As she'd repeatedly told him, none of it was any of his business. She was obviously perfectly capable of taking care of herself. He wasn't responsible for her in any way. Yet hammering away inside him was the conviction that for some unfathomable reason it *was* his business and she *did* need his protection.

He'd never felt anything like it before, he thought grimly as she uncrossed her impossibly long bare legs and put her hands on the arms of the chair. He certainly didn't *want* to feel anything like it. In fact, he'd spent the majority of his adult life avoiding precisely this kind of thing. He'd experienced enough horror, confusion and unpredictability growing up to like his life now controlled, ordered and sterile.

The way he responded to Kate threatened that. It screwed with his head and made a mockery of everything he considered vital. So he ought to just let her go. She wasn't even making it difficult. By getting to her feet, smoothing her clothes and turning to head for the door, clearly taking his silence for acquiescence, she was actually facilitating the best outcome he could have hoped for this evening.

And yet, it wasn't the outcome he wanted. Not by a long shot. He wanted her horizontal and beneath him. He wanted to spend the evening running his hands over every glorious inch of her to see if she felt as silky smooth as she looked. He wanted to find out what sounds she made when she came, and with a primal instinct he'd never have dreamt he possessed, he wanted to be the first man to make her make those sounds.

The battle for control was one he was losing with increasing momentum. The desire thundering through him had grown too powerful to ignore. With every step she took away from him his self-restraint slipped that bit more and he found himself caring that bit less. By the time she reached the door, a hair's breadth from walking out of his life for ever, which should have been perfectly fine but wasn't, all reason had fled. His blood pounded in his ears and his body ached unbearably, and all he could think was, so what if he did respond to her with an unfathomable intensity? Was he really going to let her walk out of here with her self-esteem needlessly non-existent, thinking no one wanted her when someone very definitely did?

Was he hell.

'Stop,' he said roughly, pushing back from his desk and standing up barely before he knew what he was doing.

At the door, her hand on the handle, Kate froze, then turned, and he saw a combination of wariness and surprise filling her expression as she watched him stride across the carpet towards her. 'What is it?'

He came to an abrupt halt a foot in front of her, close enough to see the rapid rise and fall of her chest and hear the breath hitch in her throat. Close enough to reach for her.

'There is one more thing,' he said, jamming his hands into his pockets before he could act on the instinct hammering away inside him.

'Oh?'

'You're wrong.'

She stared at him, bewilderment flickering in the shimmering cobalt depths of her eyes. 'You *don't* have a lot to be getting on with?'

'About your desirability.'

The pulse at the base of her neck began to flutter wildly. 'What?'

'Those boys were fools.'

'In what way?'

'You are very, *very* desirable.'

Her eyes widened for a moment and then she frowned. 'And you are very, *very* funny,' she said. 'Or not at all funny, actually.'

'You think I'm joking?' said Theo darkly, gripped once again by an irrational desire to locate everyone who'd ever decimated her self-esteem and string them up. 'I am *not* joking.'

'Nevertheless,' she said dryly, 'experience would suggest otherwise.'

'You have no experience.'

'Which kind of proves my point.'

'And I can prove *my* point.'

'Oh, yes?' she asked, lifting her chin an inch and arching an eyebrow. 'How?'

Now was the time to retreat, yelled the little voice of reason banging away in his head, demanding to be heard. *Now.* He'd achieved what he'd set out to do when he'd told her to stop. He'd corrected her misconceptions. His work was done. He should take a step back and reinstate some desperately needed distance.

Yet he couldn't move. Her wide-eyed innocence and intoxicating scent were drowning out that voice in his head. The tilt of her face and the challenge in her voice were tugging at a viscerally primitive part of him deep inside. And then he noticed that her breathing was rapid, shallow, that she was staring at his mouth, and now, heaven help him, she was actually leaning towards him, and as a strange feeling of fate enveloped him what little remained of his control simply evaporated.

'Like this,' he muttered, and with one quick step forwards, he took her face in his hands and slammed his mouth down on hers.

* * *

Theo moved so fast, so unexpectedly, that for a nanosecond Kate had no idea what was going on. She was too busy trying to process the seismic shift she'd experienced when he'd demanded she wait and she'd turned to see him striding towards her with the intensity and focus of a heat-seeking missile. The set of his jaw, the hot look in his eye and the gruffness of his voice had made her shiver from head to toe. When he'd stopped just in front of her, the tension emanating from him palpable, something deep inside her had flared to life and rushed through her blood, making her head spin. And then his words. Her? Desirable? Yeah, right.

She didn't know what had made her demand proof of it and she had no idea what she'd expected, but now he was touching her, holding her, *kissing* her, seemingly as if his life depended on it, and she reeled first with the shock of it and then with the electrifying notion that maybe she'd been a bit too quick to dismiss his claims about her appeal. There certainly didn't seem anything half-hearted about the searing pressure of his lips on hers and he really didn't seem the sort of man who would do anything he didn't want to do.

Maybe though, just to check that he hadn't been lying when he said he wasn't joking, she ought to stop just standing there like a flake and start kissing him back. Then she'd know.

Before her courage could fail her or her hang-ups get the better of her, Kate closed her eyes and leaned into him. She put her hands on his waist and took advantage of his sharp intake of breath to part her lips and then crush them back to his. And in that instant the chemistry that she'd been too ignorant to identify before ignited. The second their tongues touched, Theo groaned and immediately deepened the kiss, pulling her closer, sliding his tongue into her mouth and blowing her mind with his breathtaking skill.

As she kissed him back with equal intensity but significantly less skill, she was sure, liquid heat rocketed through her veins and pooled between her legs. Instinctively, she moved her hands further round his back and he tilted his hips, and when she felt the huge rock-hard length of his erection pressing into her abdomen, she suddenly wanted it inside her with a clenching, gnawing, relentless ache that obliterated what remained of her wits.

All rational thought evaporated, and as her head emptied her senses took over with stunning ferocity. She was aware of nothing but Theo, the solidity of his broad chest hard up against the softness of hers, his heady masculine scent and the intoxicating taste of his mouth. The heat emanating from his body fired the flames in hers, turning her insides to molten lava and setting off so many tiny fireworks that her knees went weak.

It was as if some sort of devastatingly powerful tropical weather system had taken up residence inside her, she thought dizzily. And incredibly, it seemed as if Theo were caught up in it too because, in response to the sensory onslaught and the increasingly incendiary kiss, Kate gave a helpless little moan and suddenly he was pushing her back against the door and trapping her there with his big hard body.

And she wasn't complaining. Why would she when she felt so alive, so on fire? When, for the first time ever, it seemed that someone desired her? She was not going to look this gift horse in the mouth, so when Theo removed his hands from her face and clamped them to her waist she granted him better access by arching her back slightly and winding her arms around his neck.

In response, with one hand he shoved her skirt up just enough to jam one hard muscled thigh between hers and with the other he undid the button of her jacket and then tugged her shirt from the waistband of her skirt. And all the while he continued with the drugging, soul-shattering kisses.

As white-hot desire pounded through her, Kate instinctively shifted her hips to grind herself against his thigh and alleviate the burning ache, and then he was sliding his hand beneath her top and up, singeing her sensitised skin, then cupping her breast and rubbing a thumb over her agonisingly tight nipple. The lace of her bra might as well not have been there because she felt the heat of his hand like a brand. The friction was unbearable yet she wanted more. So she pressed herself closer, ground her hips that little bit harder and the hot sparks of electric pleasure jolting through her were so thrilling, so exquisitely powerful that she instinctively tensed and gasped—

And the spell that wild, desperate need had been weaving around them shattered.

As if doused with a bucket of iced water, Theo instantly froze. His hands sprang off her, and with a rough curse he jerked back. He looked stunned. His eyes were black and his breathing was laboured. And as he raked his hands through the hair that only moments ago she'd been threading her fingers through, somewhere in the midst of the hazy desire and intense disappointment that he'd stopped, it occurred to Kate that, yes, he *could* look dishevelled, he *could* be thrown off balance, and oddly enough it was something of a relief.

'That was not meant to happen,' he said roughly, clearly as poleaxed by the strength of the chemistry that flared between them as she was.

No, well, obviously not, she thought, righting her clothes with shaking hands, hugely glad that the door was behind her for support since she wasn't sure her legs were up to the job. 'I'm sorry.'

His gaze shot to hers and his brows snapped together. 'What?' he growled, rubbing his hands over his face and shaking his head. 'No. You have nothing to be sorry about. I do. I overstepped the line. I apologise.'

Oh. Right. 'I thought there was no line.'

'There's a line.' His dark eyes glittered and she shivered. 'And you should go.'

'Or what?' she challenged rashly, responding to the warning she could hear in his tone before she could reflect on the wisdom of her question.

He let out a quick, humourless laugh. 'You do not want to know.'

Oh, but she *did.* 'I do.'

'No.'

'Yes.'

'Fine,' he bit out. 'If you don't go, we cross that line together and your virginity becomes history.'

For a moment his words hovered in the space between them, charging the air with electricity and tension, and then Kate swallowed hard, her heart thundering and the blood drumming her ears. Dear God. What was he saying? Did he want her that much? Or was he merely teasing?

'Are you serious?' she said hoarsely.

'Deadly.'

'You want to have sex with me?'

His eyes drilled into hers as he thrust his hands in his pockets. 'Yes.'

'Why?'

'Why?'

'Well, is this a pity thing?' she asked, accepting the mortification that surged through her because she had to make sure. 'You know, help the poor orphan virgin with her pathetic self-esteem issues? Are you still trying to prove a point?'

His jaw clenched and he looked as if he wanted

to hit something. 'No,' he grated, evidently hanging onto his control by a thread. 'You were right. I am not that altruistic. And believe me, pity is the last thing I am feeling at this precise moment.'

'I see,' she said, although really she was too bewildered, too stunned, to see anything.

'Good,' he snapped, taking a step back. 'So, for your own sake, Kate, I suggest you leave. Now.'

It was excellent advice. There was no doubt about that. The evening had taken an unexpectedly dramatic turn. Kate was so out of her depth she was in danger of drowning. With the way her head was spinning and her body was ablaze she ought to be feeling for the handle, yanking open the door and legging it to the lift, to *safety*, as fast as her trembling legs could carry her.

But she didn't want to leave. She didn't want safety. She wanted more of those wild kisses, more of the magnetic darkness and thrilling passion she could sense in him, and she wanted it all with an urgency that was breathtaking.

The strength of her feelings ought to have made her wary. Instead they were electrifying. She'd been hoping to offload her virginity for years. As unbelievable as it was, Theo appeared to be a hair's breadth from taking it, and she desperately wanted him to have it, because that attraction she'd so blithely dismissed as impossible earlier? Blazing.

So to hell with the consequences. So what if he was who he was and she was significantly less? It wasn't as if she were going to bump into him again. They quite literally operated on entirely different levels. Besides, recent events had taught her that life was short, and in all honesty she'd rather regret something she *had* done than something she hadn't.

She took a deep breath, licked her suddenly dry lips and opened her mouth to speak.

'Kate,' Theo cut in tersely, as if he was able to read her mind and found her thoughts deeply ill-advised.

'Yes?' she replied, knowing it was far too late for warnings when the decision was already made.

'Think very carefully.'

'I have.'

'Don't be a fool.'

'I know what I want.'

'I make no promises.'

'I don't want any.' Reality had no place here. 'Once is enough.'

He took a step towards her, his gaze cleaved to

hers, and her entire body began to tremble with desire, excitement and anticipation.

'Last chance, Kate,' he said, his voice so low and gravelly it scraped along her nerve-endings.

'I'm going nowhere.'

And it was at that precise moment that Theo's patience, already stretched paper thin, snapped. He'd tried to warn Kate off—repeatedly—and he'd given her every opportunity to leave. If she chose to defy him then she was just going to have to face the consequences. She was an adult. As she'd told him earlier, she was perfectly capable of making her own decisions. He was only human, as much at the mercy of scorching desire as the next man, and so, really, there was nothing else to be done.

'Yes, you are,' he muttered, grabbing her hand and peeling her off the door as he inexorably caved in to the raging need he'd been holding at bay for the last five minutes.

'Not here?' she said with a little gasp of surprise.

Up against a door? Her first time? Not a chance. 'Not here.'

'Then where? The sofa? Your desk?'

'My bed,' he said, leading her straight past all

the furniture and towards the door cleverly built into the wall and disguised as a bookcase.

'What—?' she started, pulling back a little, instinctively resisting the idea of walking into a wall, until he pushed the section he'd had constructed, the door opened and he led her through.

'Oh, wow,' she breathed, looking around the white minimalist room that was bathed in the soft light of the setting sun. 'You have a suite.'

He kicked the door shut, let go of her hand and strode past her towards the bed. 'I do.'

'It's incredible.'

'It's convenient,' he said, loosening the knot of his tie and pulling the whole thing off.

'For seducing the odd virgin who comes along?'

He looked at her. 'You're the first and you're not odd.'

'You're funny.'

'You're still talking.'

'I may be a bit nervous,' she said. 'Your bed is huge.'

Theo tossed his tie onto the armchair that sat in the corner of the room and undid the top two buttons of his shirt. 'If you change your mind— at *any* point—we'll stop.' It might well kill him, but he would.

Kate gave her head a quick shake and the relief that flooded through him was so fierce he didn't want to analyse it ever. 'I won't want to stop,' she said, staring at the wedge of his chest that was now exposed with a hunger he doubted she was even aware of. 'Especially not if you make it good.'

Good? *Good?* 'With chemistry like ours,' he said tautly, 'I won't even need to *try.*'

'Nonetheless, I'm expecting great things.'

'You don't know what to expect.'

Her lips quirked into a quick smile that for some reason stabbed him right in the chest. 'Ah, but that's where you're wrong, Theo. I've had orgasms. Good ones. However, I want more. I want fireworks.'

'Demanding,' he muttered, his pulse racing as his head filled with images of how she might have gone about achieving all those good orgasms.

'Long-suffering and impatient and *extremely* ready to get on with it.'

'Then stop talking.'

'Tell me what to do.'

'Come here.'

She walked—no, *sashayed* towards him, pulling the band out of her hair so that it flowed around her shoulders like liquid gold, and it was all he could do not to stalk over to her, pick her up and tumble her straight down onto the bed before whipping the desire into a frenzy and then sinking into her. Instead, he drummed up a modicum of control to merely pull her into his arms and capture her mouth with another kiss that blew his mind.

There was nothing mere about her response, though. It was as fierce as it had been when he'd first taken her in his arms and they'd shared the kiss that had been utterly unplanned, deeply unwise and yet stunningly hot.

Now as they devoured each other, she wound her arms around his neck and pressed herself against him, every inch of her seeming to fit to him perfectly, and the desire beating through his blood erupted.

Somewhere deep in the recesses of his mind he was aware he shouldn't be doing this, that if he knew what was good for him he would stop and put as much distance between himself and Kate as was humanly possible. He was no Prince Charming and it wasn't his job to help with her issues. God knew he had plenty of his own to fix. Besides, one touch of her and he turned into a man he didn't recognise and liked even less, a man driven by the basest of instincts, a man without control.

Yet he couldn't have stopped now even if someone had been holding a gun to his head. He wanted her with a hunger it was impossible to ignore, a hunger that had had him pinning her up against a door and forgetting his name.

He could tell himself all he liked that if it wasn't him relieving her of her virginity it would be someone else—a notion that was so distasteful it made him want to retch—or that it was just because it had been a while since he'd taken a woman to bed, but in truth…well, in truth there was no reason beyond clawing need and a desire that demanded to be assuaged.

And it would be fine, he assured himself, his muscles tightening as she slid her hands beneath the lapels of his jacket and pushed up. Kate might be innocent when it came to sex but she wasn't stupid. She knew the score. His conscience was clear on that front at least. Once it was over that would be that. He'd put her in a cab and out of his mind, and the entire evening would be consigned to history. He'd lock up the memories and throw away the key. He'd have no need for them. In the meantime, however, he was going to focus on her, on *them*, and on getting naked as soon as was humanly possible.

Breaking off the kiss, he shrugged his jacket off and it fell to the floor. 'Anyone would think you'd done this before,' he muttered thickly as she moved her hands to his shirt and started tackling the buttons while he set to work on getting her out of her skirt.

'I did once get to second base,' she murmured, her breathing all ragged and shallow. 'But that was only because of a bet.'

What? A bet? Somewhere in the recesses of his mind Theo was aware that little bombshell needed processing, but there was no way it was happening now. Not when all his blood was rushing from his brain to a different part of his anatomy entirely.

'Doesn't matter.' Kate frowned and bit her lower lip. 'This isn't working,' she said with a little growl of frustration that had him leaning away to tug on the back of his shirt and pull it over his head and off.

He let it drop on top of his jacket and a moment later her clothes and his trousers had joined the growing heap on the floor. He ran his gaze over her, taking in every incredible inch of her, her skin golden and glowing in the setting sun and, aha, there it was. The tattoo. What looked like an upside-down bird the size of a two-pound coin at her hipbone. He'd wondered. Now he knew. He did not need to know what it represented. That was not what this was about. Instead he focused on the expensive cream lace of her bra and knickers and the intriguing contrast it made with the shapeless navy suit she'd been wearing.

'This is sexy,' he said gruffly, touching her hip and tracing the lace there with his fingertips.

He heard and saw her breath hitch in her throat and the knowledge that she was turned on so easily had the blood thundering in his ears.

'Underwear is about the only thing that fits me properly,' she said raggedly. 'I like to buy the good stuff.'

She had excellent taste, but— 'Lose it.'

'Help me,' she breathed. 'I'm all fingers and thumbs.'

Gritting his teeth against the pounding desire, Theo put his hands on her shoulders and turned her around. He unclipped her bra and he slid it off her, then swept her hair to one side and pressed his mouth to the spot where her neck met her shoulder. She shivered. Dropped her head against his shoulder and leaned back, and the sigh she let out hit him right in the chest.

He closed his eyes, the scent of her filling his head, and almost of their own accord his hands moved slowly down her back and then round, beneath her arms, to cup her breasts. As he took the heavy weight in his palms, she gasped softly and arched her back, which pushed her breasts further into his hands and her bottom into the hard, aching length of his erection, and it took everything he had to stay where he was instead of where he wanted to be.

He swore, low and guttural, the word smothered by her skin, as desire surged to an almost agonising level. While he continued to tease her breast and nipple with one hand, he stroked the other down the smooth silky planes of her torso, her abdomen, until he slipped it beneath the lace of her knickers and reached the soft curls at the juncture of her thighs. At the intimacy of his touch she tensed for a second, and he stilled.

'Want me to stop?' he murmured, hoping to God she didn't.

'Don't you dare,' she breathed, backing up her words by opening her legs and gripping his forearm.

He parted her with his fingers and stroked, and she was so wet, so hot, it nearly unravelled him. But she hadn't done this before, at least not with anyone else. He had to go slowly, be gentle and give her time to adjust, however much it killed him. He would not be that man who lost control and shoved her up against a door.

Abandoning her breast, he took her chin and turned her head slightly and kissed her, while lower he slipped first one finger into her slippery heat and then another. Slowly he rubbed and stroked, feeling her tremble, hearing her sigh and gasp, and automatically registered her responses. When she moaned into his mouth, then whimpered, however, the sound of it blitzed his brain and he couldn't help moving his fingers that little bit faster, that little bit harder.

One of her hands shot up to the back of his head and her kisses grew frantic. Her other hand covered his, urging him on, moving him exactly where she wanted him. Her hips twisted, minutely at first, then more frenziedly and suddenly she was wrenching her mouth from his, crying out and clenching around his fingers and it was so sexy, so intense, that Theo nearly came right along with her.

CHAPTER FOUR

KATE WAS STILL tumbling down from her first orgasm given to her by someone else when her legs were whipped from beneath her and she was picked up as if she weighed nothing. Her head was still spinning. Her entire body was still quivering, and little darts of ebbing pleasure kept shooting through her, and they hadn't even got round to the actual virginity-taking part of the evening yet.

But as Theo deposited her on the bed and then turned his attention to the drawer of the bedside table, the heat dissipated and the fireworks faded. With every second that ticked by she became aware that she was lying there naked and exposed and vulnerable, and the insecurities that had been nowhere to be seen moments ago kicked in.

It wasn't that she was ashamed of the wild, desperate abandon with which she'd responded to him. She wasn't. At least, not much. It was more that she'd been so caught up in the way he'd made her feel she hadn't given her body a moment's thought beyond the pleasure it was experiencing. And then there was the fact that from the moment she'd started shedding her clothing at no point had Theo been able to look at her properly. To judge.

But with her sprawled across his bed like this, he could now, and she couldn't help wonder what he would think. There was just so much of her. She might have the height of a supermodel but she did not have the frame. She had padding. What if there was too much? Best not to let him see, she decided, scooting beneath the sheets and clutching them to her chest, then watching him take a foil packet out of the drawer and rip it open.

Of course, in terms of surface area there was way more of Theo, but in his case that wasn't a negative because he was quite the sight for sore eyes. She'd been right in her assessment of how hard he'd be. He had muscles everywhere. They rippled across the breadth of his shoulders and flexed in his strong powerful thighs. And she didn't have to wonder about where else he might have a smattering of hair any longer. She could see it sprinkled across the lean planes of his chest, then narrowing down to the erection onto which he was now rolling the condom with what looked like impressive efficiency although what did she know?

Moments ago, all that hardness and strength had been rubbing up against her back, the friction driving her wild. With any luck it would be soon rubbing up against her front, driving her even wilder. Assuming he didn't change his mind about the whole virginity-taking thing, of course. Which was a possibility because really he was out of her league in every single way. He might well take one proper look at her, wonder what on earth he was doing and leave her there feeling like a fool. And quite honestly, she wouldn't blame him.

'Stop it,' Theo muttered, his voice low and rough.

Jerked out of her madly oscillating thoughts, Kate lifted her gaze to his and saw that he was looking at her, his eyes dark and his face tense. 'Stop what?'

'Whatever it is you're thinking.'

Flushing, she bit her lip and glanced across at the curtainless windows. 'Is there some way of shutting out the light?'

'No.'

Right. 'Would you mind closing your eyes, then?'

'Yes. I would.'

'In that case, I'll just have to close mine.'

He stood there before her, enviably unselfconscious, and regarded her thoughtfully. 'You have no idea how much I want you, do you?'

'Well, I guess…that…is some sort of indication,' she said, waving a hand in the direction of his erection and vaguely wondering how on earth something of that length and girth was supposed to fit, 'but seeing as I have nothing to compare it with, no, not really.'

'You will.'

He leaned down, putting one knee on the mattress, and as he came down beside her he tugged the sheet down to her waist. When she tried to grab it back he took her wrists and held them to the bed. He ran his gaze over her for one long slow moment and a rush of heat surged through her. Her nipples tightened and a fresh ribbon of desire began to unfurl deep inside her.

'You are stunning,' he murmured and she wished she could believe it. At least he hadn't called her beautiful. If he'd done that she'd have known he was lying. 'And I am extraordinarily attracted to you,' he added gruffly, 'so stop worrying.'

Easier said than done. But the physical responses he aroused in her body did seem to obliterate her self-consciousness and whitewash her mind, so maybe she ought to trust it would work again. 'Make me,' she breathed, and he didn't need asking a second time.

Bending his head, Theo kissed her long and hard, and as she'd hoped, as before, her insecurities faded, and rational thought gave way to something primal, instinctive and way beyond her control.

As he continued his devastating assault on her mouth she softened inside with renewed need. He lowered himself, twisting slightly so he lay half on top of her, and the deliciously heavy weight of him pressed her down. So much strength and power, she thought giddily. So contained. And as for his scent, that was a dizzying combination of spice and wood and something she couldn't identify but tugged at a spot deep inside her.

Swept up in a maelstrom of desire and heat, and feeling slight and feminine for the first time in her life, Kate moaned as she kissed him back and writhed against him in a desperate, instinctive effort to get closer.

With a harsh groan, Theo tore his mouth from hers and moved it to her breast, and if she thought the sensations had been stunning when he'd touched her there earlier they were nothing compared to the electricity that zinged through her at the heat and feel of his mouth.

She clamped a hand to the back of his head and let out a strangled gasp as her stomach liquefied. He turned his attention to her other breast and as the desire rocketed through her with ever-increasing intensity, the need to touch him back became overwhelming.

She wanted to explore him. Everywhere and at length. With her hands and her mouth. She wanted to learn the texture of his skin and the strength of his muscles. She wanted to see if she could drive him as crazy as he was driving her. She'd read books. She'd seen films. She had a fairly good idea of what to do.

But what if she did it wrong? niggled the tiny voice in her head that managed to penetrate the chaos. He'd implied he wanted her a lot, and it certainly seemed that way, but what if her clumsy, naïve attempts put him off? What if he *laughed*? She couldn't risk it. And besides, she was getting impatient. Theo's kisses and caresses were divine but she wanted more. She *needed* more. Deep inside she actually ached.

The sheet that before had acted as a shield was now just in the way. It was stopping her from feeling the whole length of his body against hers, and she wanted it gone. She wanted nothing between them, not even air. So beneath him she wriggled and struggled, kicking at the fine white cotton, and Theo froze.

'What's wrong?' he said sharply, instantly lifting himself off her, and staring down at her, his eyes blazing. 'Do you want to stop?'

'Stop?' Kate muttered with a frown. 'Why would I want to stop?' Nothing short of Armageddon would make her want to stop now. Maybe not even that.

'Then what's the matter?'

'The sheet. I'm trying to get rid of it.'

'Are you sure?'

'Never been more so.'

'Thank God for that,' he breathed, yanking it off her and tossing it to one side.

Finally free, Kate bent her leg and, turning slightly, pressed her pelvis to his, her body clearly knowing how to ask for what it wanted. And Theo seemed to get it because he put a knee between her thighs and nudged her legs apart, and then he was between them, looming over her, his jaw clenched and his face dark and tight.

She could feel him at her entrance and she caught her breath, her pulse racing. It was about to happen, she thought, her entire body trembling and her heart swelling with a giant tangle of emotions she couldn't begin to unravel even if she wanted to. It was finally about to happen. After all these years. After everything...

She let her knees drop, parting her legs even wider, and then he was sliding into her, inch by incredible inch, giving her time to adjust to the strange feeling of being stretched and filled.

'Oh, my God,' she breathed, when he was embedded in her, deep and hard and strange.

'Are you all right?' he muttered harshly.

She took a moment to think about it. It might feel odd, but it hadn't hurt. She was getting used to it, and the promise of what he could do to her, how he could make her feel, bloomed inside her. 'Extremely all right,' she said, the desire and excitement building all over again at the thought of the pleasure to come. 'You?'

'Fine.'

Fine? Just *fine*? Oh, well. He had done this before. It was only momentous for her. Nevertheless, she sighed deeply and he grimaced.

'Don't move,' he said roughly.

'Why not?'

'Because if you do this will be over before it's begun.'

Oh. 'It was just a sigh.'

'That's all it'll take.'

He really wanted her that much? Perhaps he did. She could feel him pulsating deep within her. She could see the tension in his face and straining of his muscles. He looked as though it was taking every drop of his control to hold back, and it wasn't what she wanted. It wasn't what she needed.

'What if I can't help it?' she said, the ache spreading through her body demanding release with an insistence that was impossible to ignore.

'Try.'

'Impossible. Sorry.' It was too much. The need gnawing away inside her was too strong to control. Her hips shifted of their own accord, and Theo groaned.

'Heaven help me,' he said through gritted teeth before lowering his head and kissing her fiercely as he slowly withdrew, dragging along all her nerve endings, sending new thrills of desire coursing through her, and then plunged back into her.

The rhythmic pull and push of his movements stoked the flames inside her, melting her bones and boiling her blood. Her hands somehow found their way to his shoulders and she could feel his muscles shift beneath her palms with every strong powerful thrust of his body.

He was blowing her mind, and within minutes her breath was coming in short sharp pants, her heart was thundering so hard it could well escape and all she could think about was racing towards a finishing line that was simultaneously rushing towards her.

Stifling a sob of desperation, Kate wrapped her arms round Theo's neck and her legs round his waist, and it must have been the right thing to do because suddenly he was moving faster and harder, pounding into her over and over again, pushing her higher and higher, until the unbearable tension within her snapped and, with a cry, she shattered.

White-hot pulses of pleasure, stronger and more powerful than anything she'd ever experienced, barrelled through her body. Stars exploded behind her eyelids and lit up her nerve-endings. She felt as if she were falling apart, and it was so intensely incredible that she barely registered Theo letting out a tortured groan, thrusting one last time and then burying himself deep and pumping into her over and over again.

As he collapsed on top of her and they lay there for a moment, all ragged breath, pounding hearts and long sweaty tangled limbs, Kate reeled with the intensity and magnificence of it all.

She'd done it, she thought, feeling weak, limp and completely wrung out. She'd actually done it. She wasn't frigid. She wasn't undesirable. All those years of disappointment and rejection, wiped right out. All those horrible mean comments, wrong.

The enormity of everything that had happened this evening suddenly struck and emotion welled up inside her, a swirling mix of relief and triumph, inexplicably tinged with guilt and sorrow, so massive, so overwhelming that she felt a tear escape and trickle down her temple.

But this really wasn't the time or the place to dissolve into a puddle, she told herself, choking off a sob and blinking frantically as Theo carefully levered himself off her and rolled onto his back. She'd save that for the privacy of home. Right now she needed to act as if everything was fine. Deep breaths and composure. That was what was called for here.

'So that exceeded my expectations,' she said

huskily, with a nonchalance that sounded almost genuine.

'Good.'

'Thank you.'

'You're welcome.'

She thought she detected a note of aloofness in his voice that was at odds with the gruff impatience that had dominated his tone for the last half an hour, and glanced over. He was staring at the ceiling, and gone was the raw passion and the fevered tension, she saw. His expression didn't bear even the hint of a reaction to what had just happened. He certainly wasn't about to collapse into a quivering heap as she was. He was back in control, and this whole mad little interlude was over.

'So...ah... I should probably, really, go now,' she said, keen to leave before the situation could get any more awkward but unsure of the etiquette.

'You should,' he said, pushing himself up off the bed and, with barely a backwards glance, heading in the direction of what she presumed was the bathroom. 'Get dressed and I'll call you a cab.'

Kate spent much of the following forty-eight hours either breathlessly reliving the earth-shattering encounter with Theo in his office in gloriously vivid Technicolor or being battered by the emotions she'd managed to stave off when lying there in his bed.

At home, there was no one to witness the moments she drifted off into a sizzling daydream from which she generally emerged hot, flushed and trembling. Or the occasions when muscles she never knew she had twanged and she suddenly felt so vulnerable, so raw, it brought a lump to her throat and tears to her eyes. Alone, safely cocooned within her own four walls, she had no need for defences, which was just as well because any she might have mounted would have been crushed within seconds. The enormity of what had happened—not to mention the speed and unexpectedness of it—was simply too overwhelming.

She couldn't stop thinking about what it meant. She was no longer a virgin, was the bewildering, incredible realisation that kept ricocheting around her mind while she pottered about her flat achieving very little. She was no longer unusual. Well, not on *that* front, at least. She was still a great, unwieldy giant, and the boost that Theo's rampant need had given her would no doubt fade, but losing one's virginity was a rite of passage others took for granted and she'd finally made it.

And now she had, it was as if a light had suddenly switched on in her head, illuminating the shadows and making sense of things that deep down she'd always found baffling. Such as why she'd never found anyone willing to date her when out of a potential population of millions *surely* there would have been someone somewhere. It wasn't even as if she were particularly fussy, so how come she'd never met a single man who'd been up for it?

Maybe she just hadn't looked hard enough, she thought now. In fact, maybe she hadn't looked at all. Maybe it had been easier, safer, to resign herself to the status quo. Maybe she'd even become accepting of it. *Happy* with it.

And when she asked herself why that might be, it began to dawn on her that when she'd told Theo about the relationship between her height and her virginity she hadn't furnished him with the whole truth. What she hadn't revealed, what she hadn't even *known* at the time, was that for years she'd been scared. Of sex. Scared of doing it wrong and making even more of a fool of herself than she already felt.

It was so obvious now she could see it from the

other side. When she forced herself to look back to her troubled adolescence, to the time when her school friends had started losing their virginity and talked about it in great detail, she remembered she'd been fascinated and so excited about her turn, so desperate to be normal and fit in.

But when her turn never materialised, when it became apparent that she would always be on the outside, always rejected, she'd become quieter and had hidden her embarrassment and shame behind an air of mystery. Over the years that embarrassment and shame had escalated and had eventually turned into fear, which had put her off even more, creating a vicious circle that she hadn't even been aware of and which had possibly spread to other areas of her personal life, preventing her from trying new things in case they didn't work out and she made even more of an idiot of herself in the process.

But she'd had nothing to fear. Sex with Theo had been incredible. And momentous. And not only because she'd finally got rid of her virginity at the grand old age of twenty-six. Didn't it also prove that even though she would probably never be normal and would most likely never fit in, she might just *not* make a fool of herself? Theo certainly hadn't laughed at her, and he'd seen her stripped of not just her clothes but also of the protective shield she'd always kept wrapped round her.

So what was she going to do going forward? Was she really going to spend the rest of her life not trying things, just in case? Didn't that seem a bit of a waste? And hadn't there already been too much waste of life in the Cassidy family?

Surely she owed to it to herself, to her parents and her siblings, to make the most of what she had. To live life to the max. She'd allowed her virginity to hold her back by tethering her to a time of her life dominated by painful memories and teenage angst for too long.

Well, no more.

Now she'd recognised her fears she was going to confront them and let them go. So there'd be no more hiding. No more slouching. No more trepidation about the unknown. She was going to pull her shoulders back and hold her head up high as she sallied forth. She was going to be brave and bold and fabulous, and nothing was going to stop her.

CHAPTER FIVE

A MONTH LATER, Kate made herself a mint tea and took it into the sitting room to sit cross-legged on the sofa. It was one thing deciding to hold your head up and your shoulders back while you blazed a trail, she thought wretchedly, quite another to put it into practice. Because not only had it become apparent that decade-old deep-seated issues couldn't be wiped out quite as effortlessly as she'd assumed, but also life really did have the habit of suddenly walloping you about the head when you least expected it.

And to think that everything had been going so well. Theo, clearly a man of his word as well as action, had wasted no time in instructing his lawyers, and in the aftermath of a flurry of correspondence between her and his legal team, the monstrous debt her brother had accrued had been paid off and the fund Theo had promised for her sister had been set up.

As she'd hoped, the worries that had been hanging over her like the sword of Damocles disappeared in an instant and the relief was inde-scribable. Her home was safe and she'd been able to give up her extra jobs, and she had no regrets. Every time she visited her sister and saw how happy and settled she was, she knew she'd done the right thing, even if her visit the first Sunday after That Friday had momentarily shaken that conviction.

'Those are pretty,' she'd said to Milly, spying the huge bouquet of yellow roses sitting on the windowsill having dumped her bag on a chair and given her sister a hug.

'They're my favourite.'

'I know. But where did they come from?'

'Theo.'

At the mention of his name her pulse had leapt and questions had spun around her head but her smile hadn't faltered. 'That's nice.'

Milly had grinned. 'He's very good-looking, isn't he? He said he was a friend of Mike's. I liked him.'

And then her smile *had* faltered. 'He came here?'

'Yes.'

'When?'

'Yesterday.'

'What did he want?'

'To find out what my favourite flowers were.'

'Anything else?'

'I don't think so. I don't remember.'

The conversation had turned to the series Milly was watching on Netflix but Kate hadn't been able to focus. She'd been too concerned about why Theo had really shown up. When she'd questioned the staff, however, they'd reassured her that the only instruction Theo had issued was that Milly was to have whatever she needed. Kate had been sceptical, but gradually she'd come to accept it in much the same way she'd come to accept the flush of heat she experienced every time she looked at the fresh flowers that arrived weekly and reminded her of that Friday evening.

From the man himself she'd heard nothing, nor had she expected to. He'd been very clear about what he was offering and she had no reason to doubt that, which was fine because there was no future to be had with him. Apart from above average height and intense chemistry they had nothing remotely in common, and she'd neither seen nor heard any evidence to suggest he did relationships even if they had.

She hadn't bumped into him at work, thank God. As she'd suspected they trod completely different paths, so there'd been no awkward moments in a lift and no darting into nearby cupboards in an effort to avoid him. She kept her head down and worked hard, passing her probation and being given the pay rise she'd brazenly asked for after recalling what he'd said about tall people earning more.

So far, so fabulous.

But now...

Well...

Who knew what happened now?

Taking a sip of her tea to settle her churning stomach, Kate thought of the small pile of pink and white sticks on the vanity unit in the bathroom and felt her throat tighten and her head spin.

She was pregnant.

Not sick with a stomach bug as she'd assumed two days ago when she'd rung up and told her line manager she was too ill to come in.

Pregnant.

And there was no doubt about it. Because while one test might be faulty, all ten were unlikely to be, damn them and their over ninety-nine per cent accuracy.

But how could it have happened? she wondered for the billionth time since the breakfast she'd thrown up, when her brain had finally connected the random dots of early morning nausea, a missed period and recent sex. It didn't make any sense. She was no expert but she and Theo had only done it the once and he'd used protection. She'd even watched him rolling the condom on. They were supposed to be pretty infallible, weren't they, so how? Had he done it wrong? Had he ripped it? Had it somehow been *her*?

More importantly, more *relevantly*, since it was a little late to be worrying about the hows and the whys, what was she going to do? Because she couldn't have a baby. Still riddled with issues despite her best efforts to get over them, she was a mess. She was not equipped to bring up a child. She had no support network. None of her friends had children and her sister wasn't capable of understanding her situation. She had no mother to lean on and from whom to seek advice. She didn't even have grandmothers or aunts. And what about the baby's father? She couldn't imagine Theo wanting to be involved. She couldn't imagine *what* he'd think. She couldn't even *go* there right now.

And then there was the pregnancy itself. If she thought she was large and ungainly now, imagine how she'd look in nine months' time. Whales and ships in full sail sprang to mind, and, oh, the comments she'd get, the looks... How would she stand it all?

Yet the longing she felt... The *yearning* that filled every single inch of her to bursting... She'd only known about the baby for a handful of hours, but right down to her bones she wanted it. Desperately. Her heart and mind ached with it. She was so lonely and she had so much love to give. And an even greater capacity to receive it. A baby would never judge her and find her lacking. The love they'd share would be unconditional, and the mere thought of it was so intoxicating, so powerful that it shook her to the core.

There'd already been such loss in her life, she thought, her chest squeezing as she glanced at the photo on the bookshelf, the one taken of her, her parents and her siblings at the beach twelve years ago, all beaming carefree smiles and simple happiness. Such sorrow and grief. Such heartbreak. Here was her chance to rebuild the family she'd lost. To rediscover that happiness. To love and be loved. How could she *not* take it?

And so what if she did have issues? Who didn't? She could do it. Of course she could. Thousands of women had children in challenging circumstances and, really, how challenging were hers? Now she was debt-free and Milly was taken care of she could build her resources back up. And as for help and advice, there was always the Internet. It wouldn't be easy, but if she took things one step at a time and kept her head, surely she'd be able to muddle through.

And who knew? Maybe she wouldn't even have to do it on her own. There was only one way to find *that* out. Besides, Theo had the right to know about the baby, of that she was certain. And so while he'd had no reason whatsoever to contact her, she now had a very good one to contact him.

For the last four weeks Theo had found himself flat out, with a workload of Everest-like proportions.

The acquisition of the company he'd been pursuing for months was not going according to plan. Despite putting the best brains he had on it, including his own, he still hadn't come up with a way to clear the obstacles blocking the path.

Unlike every other deal he'd done, where the other side put up the semblance of a fight but inevitably collapsed during the negotiations, this one was proving trickier. Unusually, money wasn't the issue. The offer his corporate finance team had put together was the best on the table. The problem was that the current owner, a man with solidly traditional values and an extraordinary belief that ruthlessness wasn't a necessary ingredient for success, had more than enough money and was instead primarily concerned with the personality and integrity of the potential new owner. Incredibly, he appeared to have doubts about him, Theo, in this role.

Theo wanted to acquire Double X Enterprises with a hunger that gnawed away at him ceaselessly. It would be his biggest deal to date, the biggest the world had ever seen, and when he got it, it would be enough. He'd at last be satisfied. He'd have secured his place at the top, and the restlessness and the worthlessness that had dogged him for so long would be vanquished.

So he was *not* going to let it slip through his fingers simply because Daniel Bridgeman had an issue with him personally. He might be ruthless when the situation called for it but his integrity was without question. As for his personality, the aloofness and steel that the business press attributed to him suited him just fine. He was more than comfortable with being described as an ice-cool automaton. It was entirely accurate. Emotions were dangerous. They put a person at risk in so many ways just the thought of what could happen, what had *already* happened, made him break out into a cold sweat. He'd kept a lid on his for so long he doubted he had any of the damn things left anyway.

Regardless of the obstacles, though, he'd find a way to persuade Daniel Bridgeman to give him what he wanted. The man would fold eventually. Everyone did. He just had to identify his weak spot and drive a knife through it.

And in truth, the immense workload was welcome, especially today, the anniversary of his mother's death, which still hit him with the force of a sledgehammer no matter how major the distraction. He was no stranger to twenty-hour days. He'd been working all hours since he was fourteen, when he'd figured the only way he and his mother could escape his father's brutality was by being financially independent. He'd wheeled and dealed, buying low, creating value and selling high, grafting every spare minute he had with the sole aim of making enough to set them free, his relentless drive and grim determination to succeed surging with every muffled thud, every desperate cry, every sickening silence.

No one apart from himself had expected him to have such a knack for it. He'd shown little talent for anything at school apart from truancy and brawling. Yet he'd never forget the day he'd turned sixteen and told his mother that he'd amassed one hundred thousand pounds and that they should pack their bags.

He'd never forget her reaction either. The profound relief and gratitude and the maternal pride he'd been expecting were nowhere to be seen. Instead, once she'd recovered from her shock, she'd been appalled. To his bewilderment she'd refused to leave, and no amount of pleading on his part had moved her. Stunned, unable to comprehend it and devastated by her rejection and betrayal, Theo had left alone and had barely looked back.

It had been eight years since his mother died of a brain haemorrhage that he was convinced had been caused by his father although nothing could ever be proven, but the effects of how his sixteenth birthday had played out were deep-rooted and long-lasting. He'd never understand his mother's reasons for choosing to stay with a man who hit her instead of fleeing with a son who needed her, and he doubted he'd ever be free of the irrational guilt that he'd left instead of staying and trying harder to protect her despite her rejection.

And then there was the stomach-curdling

knowledge that he bore his father's genes. As a kid he'd picked fights. As a sixteen-year-old he'd swung one proper punch that had had a devastating impact. Patterns by definition repeated themselves, and the risk that he might turn out like his father was sickeningly real.

But at least the cycle of abuse ended with him. He'd vowed never to marry, never to have children, and to never *ever* let anyone close enough to tempt him to break those vows. Even if there *was* no pattern, he couldn't be a part of anyone else's life. At least, not anyone he might be foolish enough to allow himself to care about. The consequences were too severe. He couldn't be relied upon. He let people down. And if he'd ever wished it could be any other way, well, he'd stamped out that kernel of hope and yearning many years ago before it had a chance to take root. Because in the long run everyone was better off if he remained alone.

But God, he didn't want to be alone right now, he thought, his jaw tight as he stared unseeingly at the city stretched out far below his penthouse, grey and wet beneath heavy clouds and relentless rain. Not with the darkness of his adolescence, the regrets and the guilt closing in on him on all sides. His entire body ached. His head throbbed.

The emotions he preferred to deny he had were bubbling fiercely beneath an increasingly fragile surface, and the effort of suppressing them was pushing his formidable will to its limit.

Right now, he wanted to forget who he was and what he could never have. He wanted to forget everything. He wanted to lose himself in the oblivion of a warm body, long limbs and soft sighs. But not just anyone. He wanted Kate.

For weeks he'd buried the memories of the evening she'd spent in his bed. He'd put her in that taxi, set his lawyers to work, and that had been that: funding in place, desire assuaged, problem solved, the details shoved away in a corner of his brain and left to gather dust.

Today, however, with his iron-clad defences suffering a battering and the string of sleepless nights catching up with him, the memories were pushing through the cracks and invading his thoughts in scorching, vivid detail. He kept remembering the silk of her skin and the sounds she'd made. The taste of her mouth and the heat of her body. Her courage, her loyalty and her vulnerability and, most of all, the way that when they'd been talking she'd briefly made him forget who he was.

And he wanted it all again. He wanted *her*

again. With a clawing ache that had his body as hard as stone and was becoming increasingly unbearable.

However, he was just going to *have* to bear it because while he could want all he liked, there was no way he was going to actually seek Kate out. He would not be that weak. One night was all he ever allowed himself. Two with the same woman represented the kind of risky behaviour he'd always spurned. He would not indulge it. Nor would he ever again put himself in a position that demolished his control, because without control, what was he? He didn't want to know.

The grim turmoil of today would pass. It always did. He just had to get through what was left of it. Tomorrow he'd be back on track and unassailable for another three hundred and sixty-four days. In the meantime, he'd find solace in work. While many who'd grown up in similar circumstances to his had found oblivion in drugs and alcohol, he'd always found it in the pursuit of success. It had worked for him for the past sixteen years. It would work for him now.

Setting his jaw, Theo swivelled his chair round. In the drawer of his desk he found a packet of painkillers, popped the two that were left and made a mental note to buy more. He turned to one of the three screens on his desk, and was in the process of opening his inbox when his mobile rang.

'Yes?' he muttered, forcing his attention to the latest email from the head of his corporate finance team, which came with a stark lack of suggestions for how he might push through the Bridgeman deal.

'I have a Miss Kate Cassidy in the lobby,' said Bob, the concierge who manned the desk twenty-three floors below. 'She wishes to see you.'

As the information hit his brain, Theo froze. His heart slammed against his ribs and his gut clenched. His concerns about the deal evaporated and his head emptied of everything but the knowledge that Kate was downstairs, bulldozing the boundaries he'd established and breaching his space, as if in his dangerously febrile need he'd somehow conjured her up.

But he could not see her. He was too on edge, his mood too dark. Her effect on him was too unpredictable, and the last thing he wanted was to be blindsided again. So he ought to instruct Bob to send her away and keep her away.

Yet what if she *was* in trouble? What if he had her thrown out and something happened? Could his conscience bear any more guilt? No.

It couldn't. So he'd find out what she wanted, deal with it, and then get rid of her. And it would be fine. She was just one woman. He'd faced far worse. He might have once temporarily lost his mind with her, but he wouldn't lose it again. Weakness of will led to unpredictability, which led to damage and destruction, and that was unacceptable. So this time he would be prepared. This time he would be resolute and unflinching. This time would be different.

'Thank you,' he said curtly. 'Five minutes, then send her up.'

How much longer was she going to have to wait? Kate wondered as she perched on the edge of the sofa in the vast lobby of Theo's apartment building and rubbed her damp palms against her jean-clad thighs. It had already been four minutes and fifteen seconds since the concierge had told her to wait, and her nerves were shredded. Deciding to confront Theo and tell him about the pregnancy was all well in theory, but in practice it was lip-bitingly, heart-thumpingly terrifying.

How would he respond? What would he say? She'd had twenty-four hours to get used to the idea, but it was going to come as one massive shock to him. Would he be pleased? Would he be horrified? She didn't have a clue, and it was impossibly tempting to get up, spin on her heel, go home and leave it for another day.

But she wasn't going to do that, she told herself, sitting on her hands to save her nails. It went wholly against her recent resolution to be bold and brave. Besides, she had to tell him at some point, and the sooner she got it over and done with, the better. She might even be pleasantly surprised. And who knew when she'd get another chance? Just because she'd struck lucky with him being home today—a Saturday—didn't mean she would again, and it was hardly the sort of conversation she wanted to have with him at work.

So she'd wait for however long it took and try to refrain from chewing on her already raw lip. She'd admire her lavish surroundings instead. The giant dazzling chandelier that hung from the ceiling cast sparkling light across the polished marble floor and mirrored walls. The furnishings were tastefully leather and quite possibly cost more than her flat. The difference between the worlds that she and Theo inhabited could not be more marked.

What *was* he going to think?

'Miss Cassidy?' said the concierge a moment

later, his voice bouncing off the walls and making her jump. 'Mr Knox will see you now.'

Finally.

'The lift on the right will take you directly to the penthouse.'

'Thank you,' she said, mustering up a quick smile as she got to her feet and headed for said lift on legs that felt like jelly.

The doors closed behind her and she used the smooth ten-second ascent to try and calm her fluttering stomach and slow her heart-rate. It would be fine. She and Theo were both civilised adults. They might be chalk and cheese, but they could handle this. What was the worst that could happen? It wasn't as if she was expecting anything from him. She just had a message to deliver. It would be fine.

But when the lift doors opened and she stepped out, all thoughts of civility and messages shot from her head because all she could focus on was Theo.

He was standing at the far end of the wide hall, with his back to a huge floor-to-ceiling window, feet apart, arms crossed over his chest. The interminable rain of the morning had stopped and sunshine had broken through the thick cloud. It flooded in through the window, making a silhouette of him, emphasising his imposing height and the powerful breadth of the shoulders. Although clothed in jeans and a white shirt, he looked like some sort of god, in total control, master of all he surveyed, and she couldn't help thinking that if he'd been going for maximum impact, maximum intimidation, he'd nailed it.

Swallowing down the nerves tangling in her throat, Kate started walking towards him, her hand tightening on the strap of her cross-body bag that she wore like a shield. His gaze was on her as she approached, his expression unreadable. He didn't move a muscle. His jaw was set and he exuded chilly distance, which didn't bode well for what was to come, but then nor did the heat suddenly shooting along her veins and the desire surging through her body. That kind of head-scrambling reaction she could do without. She didn't need to remember how he'd made her feel when he'd held her, kissed her, been inside her. She needed to focus.

'Hi,' she said as she drew closer, his irresistible magnetism tugging her forwards even as she wanted to flee.

'What are you doing here?'

The ice-cold tone of his voice stopped her in her tracks a couple of feet away, obliterating the heat, and she inwardly flinched. So that was the way this was going to go. No 'How are you? Let me take your jacket. Would you like a drink?' He wasn't pleased to see her. He wasn't pleased at all.

Okay.

'We need to talk,' she said, beginning to regret her decision to deliver this information in person. With hindsight, maybe an email would have sufficed.

'There's nothing to talk about.'

'I'm afraid there is.'

His dark brows snapped together. 'Your sister?'

'She's fine,' she said. 'Thank you for what you did for her.'

'You're welcome.'

'Did you get my note?' Shortly after he'd fixed her finances she'd sent him a letter of thanks. It had seemed the least she could do. She hadn't had a response.

He gave a brief nod. 'Yes.'

'She loves the flowers.'

'Good.'

'It was thoughtful.'

'It was nothing.'

Right. Beneath the force of his unwavering gaze and impenetrable demeanour Kate quailed for a moment and was summoning up the courage to continue when he spoke.

'Are you in trouble?' he asked sharply.

'That's one way of putting it.'

'What?'

'Sorry, bad joke,' she said with a weak laugh although there was nothing remotely funny about any of this.

'Get to the point, Kate,' he snapped. 'I'm busy.'

Right. Yes. Good plan. She pulled her shoulders back and lifted her chin. 'There's no easy way to say this, Theo,' she said, sounding far calmer than she felt, 'so here goes. There's been a…*consequence*…to our…evening together.'

A muscle ticced in his jaw. 'What kind of consequence?'

'The nine-month kind.'

There was a moment of thundering silence, during which Kate's heart hammered while Theo seemed to freeze and pale. 'What exactly are you saying?' he said, his voice tight and low and utterly devoid of expression.

'I'm pregnant.'

The words hung there, oddly loud and blatantly unequivocal, charging the space between them with electrifying tension, and Kate wished there'd been a less impactful way of saying it because something that looked a lot like terror flared briefly in the black depths of Theo's eyes, and it made her shiver from head to toe.

'Is it mine?'

'Yes.'

'Impossible.'

'Apparently not,' she said. 'Apparently it happens.'

'How?'

'I could ask you the same question.' He did, after all, have vastly more experience than she did.

'It makes no sense.'

'I know.'

His eyes narrowed. 'Are you *sure* it's mine?'

Ouch. 'Quite sure,' she said, choosing to forgive him for his scepticism since he was clearly in a state of shock. 'I saw a doctor this morning. I'm six weeks along and I haven't had sex with anyone other than you. I could arrange a paternity test if you need proof.'

He gave his head a quick shake, although whether it was to dismiss the need for proof or to clear his thoughts she had no idea. 'Are you going to keep it?'

'Yes,' she said with a firm nod, just in case he

was thinking about persuading her otherwise. 'I am.'

'I see,' he said vaguely, and she got the impression that he'd gone to another place entirely.

'I don't expect anything from you, Theo,' she said. 'I thought you had a right to know, but that's it. It's entirely up to you how involved you would like to be. I can do this with or without you.' And it looked as if it was going to be without him because he was obviously *not* happy about it. Which was fine. 'Anyway, that's all I came to say,' she added. 'I get that it's a shock. So, take your time. Have a think about it and let me know.'

And with that, she turned on her heel and left the way she'd come.

CHAPTER SIX

HAVE A THINK?

Have a think?

How was that even possible when his safe, steady world had just been blown to smithereens? When his biggest nightmare, his greatest fear, the one he'd taken the utmost care to avoid for the whole of his adult life, had shockingly, horrifyingly materialised?

Only dimly aware of Kate's departure, Theo stood there, reeling. He couldn't move. He felt as if he were imploding. As if someone had punched in him the solar plexus and followed it up with a lead pipe to the backs of his knees. His chest was tight. His lungs ached. Dizziness descended and his vision blurred.

Breathe.

He had to breathe.

Before he passed out.

Pulling himself together, he dragged in a shaky breath and released it, and the minute the lift door closed behind Kate, he staggered back and sagged against the window.

How the hell could it have happened? he wondered numbly as he dragged shaking hands through his hair and swallowed down the nausea that surged up from his stomach. What warped twist of fate was this?

That Kate was telling the truth he didn't doubt. She'd been so calm. So matter of fact. He, on the other hand, felt as if he'd been swept up by a tornado, tossed about, and hurled back to the ground. He didn't need proof of what she claimed. He needed a drink. A damn time machine would be better. One that took him back to that evening so he could throw her out of his office instead of recklessly caving in to inexplicable desire and carting her off to his bed.

As for his involvement, well, that was a no-brainer. He wouldn't be involved at all. He couldn't. He was no good. It was highly probable he'd turn out to be worse than that. He could not be part of Kate's pregnancy or the raising of a child. Under any circumstances. He wouldn't even know how. To him the word 'father' didn't conjure up images of fishing trips and football games in the park. It represented fear and pain and desolation. He had no experience of anything different. None of the other kids he'd hung out with, kicking around the streets and causing trouble in order to avoid having to go home, had had positive father figures in their lives. He couldn't provide what a child needed. Hell, he didn't even know what that was.

All he did know was that he could not claim his child. The risks were too great. It would be in the child's best, *safest*, interests if he stayed far, far away. Emotionally. Physically. In every way that he could think of. He would not allow himself to give even a nanosecond's thought to what could be if he weren't so terrified of history repeating itself. He couldn't. The child deserved to live a life without fear.

So he would wipe Kate and the baby and the last fifteen minutes of his life from his head, and get back to the problems he *could* understand. If he focused on work and nothing else, the tightness in his chest would ease. The swirling blackness would clear. *Something* would come to him.

Although…

Hang on…

What if this latest development wasn't quite the horrendous disaster it appeared to be? What if it could, in fact, be the answer to the issue that had been plaguing him for months?

The questions slammed into his head, burying the chaos and turmoil with the cold clear logic that had rescued him from such situations many a time, and he instinctively clung onto them like a lifeline.

Were Kate and this pregnancy to become public knowledge, he thought, strength flooding back to his limbs as his brain started to teem with possibilities, it would definitely make him more palatable to Double X Enterprises' recalcitrant CEO. Especially if he stood by her. Daniel Bridgeman had been married to the same woman for fifty years. They'd had no children, but his wife was an integral part of his business. She was on the board of directors and appeared by his side at functions. He cited her as being behind every major decision he'd ever taken.

All of the above clearly indicated that the man valued such a partnership highly, so what if Theo presented one of his own? One he had readymade. Surely that would allay any concerns the other man might have about his so-called ruthlessness and his less than acceptable personality? How much more touchy-feely could you get than a partner and an imminent baby?

So what if manipulating situations and faking a relationship *did* seem to smack of the ruthlessness and the lack of integrity he was aiming to disprove? The end more than justified the means. For the deal of a lifetime, a deal he'd *needed* to push through, he could—and would—do anything.

He foresaw no problem implementing this strategy. It wasn't as if any of it were for real. Once he'd achieved his goal he'd let Kate go and they'd be done. Should she put up any resistance, he had an arsenal of weapons with which to persuade her otherwise. And presenting to the world a facade he wanted it to see was second nature to him. He'd been doing it for years, ever since he'd learned at the tender age of seven to explain away the bruises and fractures and convince anyone who asked that everything at home was absolutely fine.

It was the best, the *only*, option on the table, so, ignoring the tiny voice in his head demanding to know what the hell he thought he was doing, Theo hauled his mobile out of his back pocket, hit the dial button and strode towards the lift.

'Kate Cassidy,' he said curtly when Bob answered. 'Stop her.'

Kate had got as far as the enormous slowly revolving glass door when the concierge caught up with her. Her thoughts on the scene that had just gone down up in the penthouse were mixed. On the one hand she was relieved that she'd accomplished her mission and had escaped unscathed, yet on the other she was gutted. She wasn't sure why. It wasn't as if she'd been expecting Theo to break open the champagne. She hadn't been expecting anything. So the disappointment didn't make any sense, which was yet another entry in the ever-growing canon of things about herself she didn't understand.

'Miss Cassidy,' called the man, puffing a little as he reached her.

'Yes?'

'Mr Knox requests that you wait.'

Kate stilled, her heart irrationally giving a little leap. He wanted her to wait? Why? What could that mean? Had he changed his mind? Did he want to be involved? *What?*

Well, she was about to find out, she thought, adrenaline surging and her pulse racing as her gaze shifted to the man striding across the lobby towards her. He seemed so energised, so full of purpose now that she found it hard to reconcile this version of him with the rigidly monosyllabic one she'd left up there in his penthouse. It had only been two minutes. What could possibly have happened in the interim?

'Thank you, Bob,' said Theo to the concierge before switching his attention to her and virtually lasering her to the spot with the force of his gaze. 'Come with me.'

Before she could respond, he'd taken her elbow and was wheeling her in the direction of a room off the lobby. He led her into what was clearly a private meeting room, judging by the antique breakfast table and half a dozen dining chairs, and let her go.

'Are you all right?' she asked with a frown as she watched him close the door and then turn back to her.

'Couldn't be better.'

'I don't understand.'

'Marry me.'

Kate froze and stared at him, her jaw practically hitting the floor while her head spun. 'I—I'm sorry?' she stammered.

'You heard,' he said, something about the gleam in his eyes making shivers race up and down her spine. 'Marry me.'

'Don't be ridiculous.'

'I'm not being ridiculous.'

Her eyes widened. 'You're being *serious*?'

'Yes.'

Kate studied him closely for a moment and thought, no, well, he did look intense and steely and he wasn't the type to joke. But *marrying*? Her and *Theo*? What alternative universe was this? 'Why?'

'You're pregnant with my child.'

Okay, so there was that, but it didn't seem a likely motive in this day and age. There had to be something else behind it. But what? What could possibly have had Theo dramatically haring after her and issuing a proposal? He couldn't have suddenly realised he'd developed *feelings* for her, could he? No. That was impossible. He'd shown no sign of wanting her at any stage since he'd hustled her out of his office suite and bundled her into a taxi. Although presumably stranger things had happened. Somewhere and at some point...

Had her news jolted him into some kind of epiphany or something? He *had* been in a state of shock earlier. And he did have a reputation for knowing what he wanted, going for it and not giving up until he got it. So had she, however improbable it might seem, fallen into that category of being something he wanted?

Doubtful.

And yet...

What if this was her rock-bottom self-esteem making her assume the worst again? Just because no one had ever wanted to marry her before—or even date her, for that matter—didn't mean that no one ever would. So could Theo actually want her? For real? She had to allow that it was a possibility, for personal growth purposes, if nothing else. He *was* looking at her in a spine-tinglingly fierce kind of way. And he *had* just asked her to marry him, which he would not have done if he hadn't meant it.

So.

Maybe the circumstances were a bit of a surprise but people had married for less. Maybe she and Theo could work. Somehow. They already did on a carnal level, and imagine a lifetime of sex like that...

Hmm.

Perhaps it was best not to do that. Or get too carried away. Already excitement and a longing for what could be were drumming through her and scrambling her brain. She had to remain calm.

'Right,' she said, forcing herself to proceed with caution and fervently trying to keep the familiar fuzzy image of a cosy family unit at bay. 'I see. Well. This is rather unexpected.'

'Tell me about it,' he said, his eyes dark and his expression unreadable. 'I should clarify.'

Clarify? Yes. Good idea. 'Please do.'

'What I am about to tell you is highly confidential.'

A shiver ran down her spine as her heart thumped. Could this be because relationships between personnel at his company were discouraged? How thrilling. 'I understand.'

'I am pursuing the acquisition of Double X Enterprises.'

What? Oh. Right. Back to business. Odd. But never mind. His brain was famously nimble and at least it would give her fevered thoughts a respite. 'I'd heard.'

'It's not going as smoothly as I'd hoped,' he said, and she could hear a hint of frustration in his voice. 'To gain a competitive edge I need to acquire something I lack. To put it bluntly, a partner.'

Kate frowned. What on earth was he talking about? Why would he need a partner to seal the deal? From what she knew about him he was a lone wolf all the way. He didn't do partners. Besides, how could *she* help? She was way down the corporate food chain. And although she supposed it was flattering that he considered her a sounding board, what did any of this have to do with her and the pregnancy and his absurd yet intriguing offer of marriage?

'Would you like me to help you find one?' she asked, more than slightly bewildered.

'What? No. As I said, I want you to fill the role.'

She stared at him, still none the wiser. 'I'm afraid you've lost me.'

'I need a partner, preferably a fiancée,' he said flatly, his patience obviously stretched to the limit by her complete inability to grasp what he was getting at. 'Someone to accompany me to dinner from time to time. The odd gala or party. Lunch. Drinks.'

Huh?

'Daniel Bridgeman, the CEO of Double X Enterprises, values such a relationship so I need to provide him with one. For appearances' sake. Temporarily. Until he signs on the dotted line.'

Oh.

Oh.

As the true meaning of what he was after sank in Kate felt as if she'd been thumped in the gut. Her throat tightened and her ears began to buzz and a hot flush rocketed through her.

'Your company is all I require, Kate,' Theo

continued, evidently unaware of the devastation he was beginning to wreak on her. 'Your time and your acting skills. Nothing more. Apart from complete discretion, naturally. I anticipate it'll take a fortnight. A month at the most. I'll supply you with the necessary wardrobe and a campaign plan. All you have to do is turn up when and where I tell you, pat your abdomen and smile.'

He stopped and looked at her, clearly waiting for a response, but Kate couldn't speak for the pounding of her head and the blurring of her vision. Oh, she was an idiot, she thought, swallowing hard to dislodge the knot that had formed there and turning away to blink back the sudden sting in her eyes. Why on earth would someone like Theo be interested in marrying someone like her for real? What had she been thinking? How deluded could she still *be*? They hardly knew each other. All they'd had was a one-time thing. He hadn't changed his mind about her. Why would he?

Of course, it would have saved her a whole lot of trouble if he'd started with the business angle to the marriage proposal in the first place, but obviously it hadn't occurred to him that he needed to. Why would it have when the notion was so laughably inconceivable?

That she'd got the wrong idea was entirely her fault, and it wasn't even the first time. There'd been the occasion that evening in his office when he'd told her she was unique. For the briefest, headiest of moments she'd thought he'd been paying her a compliment, but all he'd meant was her situation—her virginity. Then, as now, she'd been stupidly filled with a hope that had been swiftly dashed, and she had nobody but herself to blame.

But while she might be naïve and hopeless, one thing was very clear. She was *not* going to be steamrollered into a fake engagement, marriage, whatever, just because it suited him. Self-esteem issues or no self-esteem issues, even she was not going to be used in that way, and there was no way she'd allow their unborn child to become a pawn in its unfortunate father's shady business deals. So she swallowed hard and stamped down on the emotions swirling around inside her.

'It's an interesting proposal,' she said, with a strength that interestingly she didn't even have to dig very deep for.

'A necessary one,' he countered.

'I see.'

'Excellent,' he said, with the flicker of a satisfied smile. 'I'll email you the details in the morning and—'

'No.'

The word was like the crack of a whip and for a moment it hovered in the silence between them.

Theo looked at her, his eyebrows lifting a fraction. 'What do you mean, no?' he said, sounding faintly taken aback, as if he was unused to hearing the word, which, she supposed, he was.

'I'm not going to do it.'

'Why not?'

She stared at him. *Why not?* She didn't know where to begin. 'Well, for one thing,' she said, opting for the least complicated reason, 'it wouldn't work. No one would ever believe it.'

'Of course they would,' he said, failure obviously a concept he was as familiar with as defiance. 'People do not tend to question me.'

Right. 'It's unethical.'

A flicker of irritation flitted across his face at that. 'It's business.'

'So find someone else.'

'I don't want someone else. I want you.'

'Because it's convenient.'

A muscle ticced in his jaw. 'Why else?'

At least he didn't bother denying it. 'Still no.'

His eyes narrowed minutely and the hairs at

the back of her neck jumped up. 'Think very carefully, Kate.'

'I am,' she said, determined not to be put off by her body's infuriating response to him. 'Do you honestly believe you can basically say you want to use me and our baby for your own selfish ends, and I'd be all, sure, why not?'

'Yes.'

'Well, you're wrong.'

His jaw tightened. 'You will be handsomely compensated for your efforts.'

'I don't want your money.'

'You were happy enough to take it a month ago.'

At that, Kate went very still, her blood chilling and her heart thudding. Why would he mention that now? 'What are you suggesting?' she asked as a ribbon of trepidation wound through her.

'Nothing,' he said, not taking his eyes off her for a second. 'Merely stating a fact.'

'Then why bring it up?'

'Why not?'

'Because it sounds like a threat.'

'How you interpret it is up to you,' he said smoothly. 'However, there is also your career to consider.'

Her stomach clenched. What did that have to

do with anything? 'My career?' she echoed, the apprehension growing.

'The ICA may take a dim view of what you get up to online, don't you think?'

'But then again, they may not.'

'I imagine it would depend on who filed the complaint and how many favours they were owed.'

'There's no need for anyone else to know.'

'I couldn't agree more.'

And there it was.

The threat she'd heard earlier.

Now not even *thinly* veiled.

As the truth of what he was saying struck her like a blow to the head Kate went from icy cold to boiling hot, numb incredulity giving way to a burning deluge of emotion.

The *bastard*.

The complete and utter rat.

How could she ever have thought he wasn't all bad? He was just as cold and heartless as she'd originally believed. She'd heard he'd go to any lengths to get what he wanted, but there was clearly no line he wouldn't cross and no weapon he wouldn't use. He'd taken everything she'd told him that evening in his office, all those deeply personal issues of hers, her troubled adolescence and her worries about her sister, the money, and turned them against her.

How could he *do* that? she wondered, her entire body shaking as the silence thundered between them. How could he stoop so low? Oh, she was *such* a fool to have shared. She should have known she'd come to regret it. If only she hadn't taken his money. If only she'd been stronger. But how could he have insisted she'd owe him nothing and then demand repayment? Had he *no* integrity?

Something inside her withered and died, and she ruthlessly squashed down the surge of disappointment and hurt and who knew what else.

'You bastard,' she said, her voice hoarse with suppressed emotion.

His mouth twisted. 'If only.'

'What you're suggesting is blackmail.'

'That's an ugly word.'

'It's an ugly concept.'

'How this plays out is entirely up to you, Kate,' he said. 'The choice is yours.'

'It's no choice at all and you know it.'

'So we have a deal?'

He made it sound like a question, but it wasn't. He had her in the palm of his hand. She so badly wanted to tell him to go to hell but there was too much at stake. While she might be willing to forfeit her career and even her home to retain the moral high ground and never have anything to do with him ever again, she was *not* risking her sister's well-being. If she didn't comply with his wishes, Theo would withdraw his funding. She was sure of it. Because his word clearly meant nothing.

So fine. She'd accompany him to the odd social event if that was what he wanted. She could dangle off his arm and smile nicely for a month. Now she'd seen a glimpse of the man behind the mask she wouldn't be taken in again. Her guard would remain well and truly up and she would never forget what a low-life jerk he really was.

'We have a deal.'

CHAPTER SEVEN

THE FOLLOWING EVENING, Kate sat at her dressing table, peering into the tiny mirror while she fastened hoops to her earlobes and wishing she were somewhere else. Like Mars. Outwardly, dressed in a gown of green satin, all made up with her hair done, she looked a picture of sophisticated serenity. Inside, she seethed.

Theo had wasted no time in putting his diabolical plan into action. This morning she'd received a brief text informing her that tonight they would be going out to a black-tie function. Half an hour later she'd been summoned to an exclusive store in Knightsbridge that catered for the exceptionally tall, where a personal shopper had revamped her entire wardrobe. She'd then been whisked to a salon and had emerged three hours later with a sleek up-do and a face full of make-up that was way more than she usually wore but at least did a good job of disguising the effects of a sleepless night and continued morning sickness.

While she'd been sitting in the chair with people flitting around and dancing attendance on her it had occurred to her that what the makeover suggested was the height of insult but then she'd expect nothing less from a man who'd coldly and calculatingly used her honesty and her hang-ups to blackmail her.

Twenty-four hours after Theo had delivered his ultimatum she still reeled with the shoddiness of it. For some reason she'd thought he was somehow *more* than his reputation would have her believe. Foolishly, she'd allowed herself to change her mind about him. She didn't know why. The evidence had been flimsy at best, and, with the benefit of hindsight, granting him attributes he clearly didn't have had been a mistake of epic proportions. She couldn't have been more wrong about any of it, and the worst thing was it was her own fault because, while he might have manipulated her, he hadn't exactly tricked her. So not only was the disillusionment hitting her hard, she also felt stupid and naïve and unable to trust her own judgement. Again.

The buzzer sounded, shattering the quiet, and Kate jumped, the simmering anger and resentment she continued to feel towards Theo flaring up deep inside her. It was show-time—but, oh, how tempted she was to lift the window, lean out and tell him to get lost. But she didn't dare risk it. She didn't trust him one little bit. Not now.

There was no need to hurry, though, was there? Keeping him waiting another five minutes might be petty, but it would also be deeply, *deeply* satisfying. So Kate calmly redid her lipstick and gave her neck another squirt of scent. When the buzzer went again, she ignored it in favour of checking her phone for messages and emails before popping it in her bag.

It was only after the third, longer, more jabbing buzz that she figured if she didn't want him storming up here and dragging her out she'd better get going. So she slipped on her shoes, locked up and went downstairs. At the end of the hall, she took a deep breath and pulled her shoulders back, and opened the front door to see Theo leaning against a car, his hands thrust into the pockets of his trousers, looking decidedly unimpressed. Which was extremely pleasing and, frankly, only fair given his lousy treatment of her.

What *wasn't* fair, though, she thought, the sharp stab of triumph fading beneath an unwelcome surge of heat and an unforgivable thump of desire as she walked towards him, was how he could look so devastatingly handsome when he was so horribly, mercilessly *awful*. His tuxedo fitted him as if he'd been stitched into it. The snowy white of his shirt highlighted the strength of his jaw and the chiselled perfection of his features. Smouldering and dangerous were the adjectives that sprang to mind and, oh, great, now she was being bombarded with images of all the things he'd once done to her.

'You're late,' he said curtly, pushing himself off the car and turning to open the rear passenger door.

Kate snapped out of her trance and inwardly bristled at the icy annoyance in his tone. 'I nearly didn't come down at all.'

'We have a deal.'

'I know,' she said before adding pointedly, 'and I, for one, don't go back on my word.'

Wrenching her gaze from his, which was annoyingly harder than it ought to be, she slid into the car with as much elegance as she could manage and settled back against the soft leather seat. A minute later Theo joined her, closing the door behind him with a soft thud, and instantly it felt as if all the oxygen had been sucked out of the air. To her horror, her breath caught in her throat and her entire body hummed with a dizzying sort of awareness. Her dress, which had fitted perfectly a moment ago, suddenly seemed impossibly tight. As he shifted on the seat she realised he was too big, too near, and he smelled too good. She wanted to climb into his lap and get all up close and personal, and see if she couldn't do something about the tired lines that fanned out from his eyes and bracketed his mouth, which was simply insane when she loathed him with every ounce of her being.

Channelling the outrage that had dominated her emotions recently, Kate kept to her side and made herself look out of her window, but it didn't block the heat of his gaze on her or the corresponding flip of her stomach.

'You look stunning.'

'Thank you,' she said, refusing to acknowledge the brief stab of pleasure she felt at his compliment.

'How have you been?'

'Busy.'

'Shopping?'

'Among other things.'

'You maxed out my credit card.'

'This body costs a lot to clothe well,' she said, 'and all this,' she added, shooting him a quick glance and waving a hand around her face and hair, 'comes at a price.'

'It was worth every penny.'

She was *not* going to respond to that. 'Yes, well, you did say the budget was unlimited,' she said. 'And given how I ended up in this particular situation, it seemed the least you could do to make amends.'

'Did it work?'

'No.'

'Unusual.'

'In what way?'

'Money tends to fix most problems.'

'But not all?'

A pause. A flash of bleakness in his eyes. 'No,' he said with a faint frown. 'Not all.'

He was obviously thinking of the deal and the obstructive Mr Bridgeman, and Kate mentally high-fived the man she'd never met but who had to be the only person on the planet to defy him.

'So what's this evening about, then?' she asked, abandoning the view of the heavy traffic of central London through which they were inching, and shifting to bestow on him her iciest glare.

'It's a fundraiser.'

'What for?'

'A charity that helps young entrepreneurs who haven't had the easiest start in life.'

'Like you?'

'How would that be like me?'

The look that accompanied his response was dark and forbidding, and she would have wondered what had caused the sudden tension radiating off him had she been remotely interested in digging deeper. 'Well, you started in business at a young age, didn't you? No handy trust fund or Oxbridge education.'

The tension eased. 'Yes.'

'A worthy cause.'

'Very.'

'Who's going to be there?'

'Business acquaintances mainly.'

But no friends. *How* unsurprising. 'The CEO you're trying to sweeten?'

'No. He's away.'

Oh. 'Doesn't that rather defeat the object of the exercise?'

'Not at all. Tonight is about building a narrative and spreading your news.'

Her news, she noted. Not *their* news. Right now she was useful to him, the means to an end, but once it was done she'd be on her own and she must never forget it. 'Why are you so keen to impress him?'

'I want his business.'

'I know, but why doesn't he want to sell it to you?'

'He has concerns.'

'About what?'

'My personality,' he said with a faint grimace that she found enormously satisfying. 'My integrity.'

Really? Hah. There were clearly no flies on this Mr Bridgeman. 'He knows you well.'

'We've never met.'

'Then he disapproves of your reputation.'

'Apparently so,' he said, as if he found it impossible to believe that anyone would dare.

'Astounding.'

'Quite.'

'Don't you think faking an engagement to facilitate a business deal falls somewhat short of the integrity you're keen on showing him you have?'

His jaw tightened and his expression hardened. 'Once the papers are signed it won't matter.'

Did he really mean that? He must. After all, she had direct experience how single-minded and immovable he could be when he wanted something, didn't she? 'How long do you think it's going to take?'

'As long as is necessary.'

'What if the deal never comes off?'

'That's not going to happen.'

Hmm. 'Yes, well, while your confidence is impressive,' she said, managing to inject a pleasing note of disdain into her voice, 'I'd be happier if we put a time limit on things.'

He arched one dark eyebrow. 'Conditions, Kate?'

'It's a fair one, you have to admit.'

'You're in no position to negotiate.'

Damn. He had her there. 'So that's a no?'

'That's very much a no.'

Then she'd better put her back into this ridiculous farce so that Daniel Bridgeman sold Theo his company asap and she could get on with her life. 'I have another one,' she said coolly. 'One that's not as easy to dismiss.'

'Oh?'

'I might have agreed to this little charade, fake engagement, whatever, but I do not consent to kissing or inappropriate touching or anything else like it.'

For a moment Theo didn't respond. Instead, his gaze dropped to her mouth and for some reason the temperature inside the car rocketed. Her head spun and her mouth went dry and an unforgivable punch of lust hit her in the gut.

'I wasn't aware I'd asked you to,' he said, sounding so in control, so uninterested, she envied him.

'Just making sure.'

'I'll keep it in mind.'

And she ought to keep in mind the reason she was here—the blackmail. 'So my job is to enhance your personality and show Mr Bridgeman your softer side?' she said, pulling herself together and focusing.

'Yes.'

'A Herculean task when you don't have one.'

'I have no doubt you are up to the challenge.'

'Aren't you concerned I might muck it up?'

'Why would you do that?'

'I've never had a boyfriend, let alone a fiancé.'

'You're a quick learner,' he said, something about his tone heating her blood and melting her stomach despite her resolve to remain cool and aloof. 'You'll soon pick it up.'

Kate thought of glaciers and straightened her spine. 'How do you know I'm not planning to sabotage things in revenge for the way you blackmailed me into this?'

'Are you?'

'I might be.'

'I wouldn't,' he said mildly, although she could hear his warning loud and clear.

'If only I still had my virginity to sell,' she said wistfully, half meaning it.

'Regrets?'

'Do you care either way?'

Something flitted across his expression, but it was gone before she could even try and identify it. 'No.'

'No, well, why would you?' she said, feeling the tiniest bit stung despite herself. 'When you own the world, I guess you don't need to worry so much about other people's feelings.'

'I guess not,' he agreed impassively.

'So brusque,' she said with a shake of her head. 'So serious. So *steely*.'

'Is that a problem?'

'Not particularly, although I guess it depends on your perspective. It seems to me, though, that a real girlfriend might expect the occasional smile. A fiancée definitely would, I should think.'

'How would you know?'

Ooh, that was harsh. But fair, she grudgingly had to admit. 'Well, what do *you* think?'

'Me? I have no idea.'

She stared at him, surprise momentarily nudging everything else out of the way. 'None?'

'None.'

'But you must have had a girlfriend.'

'Must I?'

'Haven't you? *Ever?*'

'I don't have the time.'

Oh, dear.

She'd assumed at least Theo would know what he was doing, but it now seemed as though it was a case of the blind leading the blind. How had he thought this approach would ever work? Was he nuts?

'Right,' she said, resenting him even more for putting her in this position. 'Well. Let's hope I'm not the only one who's a quick learner.'

Four hours later, having escaped to the bathroom after interminable drinks, a sumptuous six-course dinner and an auction of promises during which the extravagant luxury of the lots and preposterous figures whizzing around had blown her mind, Kate was exhausted. Keeping a smile fixed to her face and gazing at Theo in adoration when all she wanted was to stab him with a hairpin was draining.

He was not playing fair. Having no intention

of giving him any reason to think she wasn't doing her best and therefore renege on his side of the bargain, she had thrown herself into her role. Theo, on the other hand, had not. He'd introduced her as his pregnant fiancée, and remained by her side, but that was pretty much it. He hadn't smiled at her. He'd barely even looked at her. She'd had to do all the work, and once tonight was over they were very definitely going to be having words.

Unexpectedly, however, there had been *some* positives to the evening. After the initial flurry of interest, Kate had become pretty much invisible, which was a novelty. Everyone was far more interested in the man at her side. His appearance in public was apparently something of a rarity, and, despite his giving off such chilly vibes he could cause frostbite, people couldn't get enough of him. The awe he was held in and the resultant fawning she witnessed made her stomach turn, but at least it meant she could observe instead of being observed for once.

And then there was the fact that he stood nearly a head above her. She had no need to slouch or try and make herself smaller. She could pull her shoulders back and hold herself straight and amazingly she still only just reached his chin.

She might tower over everyone else but at Theo's side, for the first time ever, she felt normal. So normal, in fact, that next time they went out she might even wear a pair of the heels she hadn't been able to resist adding to the pile of new clothing she'd accumulated this morning.

Of course there'd also been some negatives, because unfortunately her body still hadn't got the memo about what a despicable human being Theo was. Her body kept wanting to take advantage of the fake engagement and, well, *snuggle*. So much so that she found herself actually regretting the no kissing and no contact condition of hers, which was wrong on practically every level there was.

At least the evening was coming to an end. She couldn't wait to get home and collapse into bed. She had the feeling that the continued attraction she felt, so obviously now one-sided, was going to become increasingly hard to handle, and she could only hope that Daniel Bridgeman got wind of the 'engagement', was fooled into thinking Theo's unfortunate personality had undergone a one-hundred-and-eighty-degree change, and announced his plan to go ahead with the deal just as soon as was humanly possible.

What she *couldn't* do was stay in here, much

as she wouldn't mind taking a quick nap, because the door to the bathroom had just opened and people had come in, no doubt wishing to use the stall she was occupying.

Fighting a yawn and rolling her head to ease the kinks in her neck, Kate pulled herself together. She stood up and smoothed her dress, and was just about to slide the lock when something about the conversation on the other side of the door made her go very still.

'Yes, but who *is* she?' she heard one woman ask, the incredulity in her voice as clear as a bell.

'Apparently she works for him.'

'Theo Knox dipping his nib in the company ink? That doesn't sound like him.'

'I agree. But, well, it wouldn't be the first time a woman has trapped a man into marriage by getting pregnant, would it?'

'I guess not.'

'So, Miss Cassidy, what was it about gorgeous billionaire Theo Knox that first caught your eye?'

'Why, his sparkling personality, of course.'

Catty laughter.

A pause.

What sounded like a rummage in a handbag.

Then, 'No ring, I noticed.'

'I noticed that, too.'

'And he's not exactly *doting*, is he?'

'Well, would you be? Have you seen the size of her? She's huge.'

'I *know*.'

'Do you really think the baby's his?'

'No idea. Pass me a tissue, would you?'

The conversation stopped and then came the vague sounds of make-up being reapplied but Kate barely registered any of it. Her head was spinning, her heart was racing and she was trembling from head to toe. Every word had slammed into her, leaving her battered and bruised and sore. She didn't know why. Logically, they should not affect her. Her engagement to Theo was fake. She wasn't a gold-digger. She most certainly didn't want him to dote.

But they did. For some reason, they did. They sliced right through her and ripped her open, brutally exposing her innermost vulnerabilities and stabbing straight at them. When would she stop being a freak show? When would someone want her for real? What had she ever done to deserve any of this?

Her eyes stung and her throat tightened—blasted hormones—but she summoned up strength from somewhere deep inside and took a long, steadying breath, because *she* knew the truth. The gossip and these women meant nothing. And yes, she was abnormally tall, but there wasn't anything she could do about it, so she could either crumple in a heap of self-pity or let it go, and, frankly, this dress was too gorgeous to ruin.

Mind made up, she briefly looked up at the ceiling and blinked rapidly to dispel the threat of tears, then pulled her shoulders back and set her jaw. Clinging onto her courage as if her life depended on it, she opened the door, walked to a basin to wash her hands and, with a wide beam at the two bitchy women who stared at her in dawning shock and horror, sailed out.

CHAPTER EIGHT

BACK AT THE table that Kate had left fifteen minutes ago, Theo rolled a tumbler of thirty-year-old single malt between his fingers and tuned out of the conversation going on around him to run a quick assessment of the evening. Socialising was not his forte. He loathed small talk and sycophancy as much as he abhorred the idea of the press poking into his background and his personal life. However, things had gone well tonight, and he had no doubt that the news of his newly altered civil status would soon reach the right ears.

Despite her vague threat to sabotage his plans, Kate had embraced the role of fiancée admirably, although he could have done with fewer of her dazzling smiles and the occasional touches to his arm. Each of the former momentarily blinded him and each of the latter sent stabs of electricity shooting through him.

His irritatingly intense response to her was the only fly in tonight's ointment, and would have been a whole lot easier to ignore if he weren't so constantly aware of her. When she'd emerged from her building earlier, wrapped in green satin and looking so spectacularly sexy he'd gone as hard as granite, his gut instinct had been to grab her hand and take her back upstairs. In the car, which he'd always considered roomy, he'd had to fight for air. Her understandable spikiness, which ought to have doused the desire rocketing through him, had only intensified it.

But he'd held it together then and he was holding it together now. No one had any inkling of the battle that had been raging inside him all evening, and it would stay that way. Even if Kate hadn't imposed that no kissing, no inappropriate touching condition on their relationship, which now, perversely, was all he could think about, there was too much at stake to crack. He could not, and would not, concede even a millimetre of ground to anyone, let alone a woman who had once rendered him so unacceptably weak. Nevertheless, the tension gripping him was draining, and the minute Kate returned they'd leave. He'd drop her home and initiate the next step in the plan because, now, this evening, their work was done.

And here she was, he thought with a familiar

bolt of heat, his gaze instinctively finding her as she wove sinuously between the tables towards him. Beneath the low, warm light of the chandeliers, she shimmered. Her hair gleamed and her skin glowed and the overall effect was irritatingly dazzling. But as she drew nearer, something struck him as wrong. The rest of her might be glowing but her face was pale. Her smile was too tight and no amount of smoky eye make-up could mask the fact that her eyes were overly bright.

Without even thinking to question why any of this was relevant, Theo abandoned his drink and got to his feet. He strode over to intercept her and took her elbow to draw her to one side, leading her through the French doors that opened onto the torch-lit terrace and into the warm jasmine-scented shadows. To his alarm, she didn't protest.

'What's the matter?' he said, noting the taut rigidity of her body and wondering whether it had anything to do with the pregnancy he was finding unexpectedly difficult to ignore.

She swallowed hard and stared at the ground an inch to his right. 'Are we done here?' she said, her voice strangely hoarse. 'Because I'd like to leave.'

Theo frowned and thrust his hands in the pockets of his trousers. 'Are you all right?'

'Of course.'

'Tired?'

'I'm always tired.'

'So what's different?'

'It's not important.'

Frustration speared through him. How could he help if he didn't know what was wrong? 'Anything that might affect what I'm trying to achieve here is important.'

'Ah, yes,' she said with a bitterness he found he didn't like. 'It wouldn't do to forget that.'

'What happened?'

'Nothing happened.'

'Tell me.'

'Okay, fine,' she said, sighing in exasperation as she *finally* looked at him. 'We're fooling no one with this whole fake engagement thing, Theo.'

'Oh?' he said, the hurt in her eyes that she was trying so hard to hide hitting him in the gut and for some reason knocking him for six.

'Apparently I'm a gold-digger who's played the oldest trick in the book and trapped you into marriage by deliberately getting pregnant.'

What the hell? 'According to who?'

'Some women I overheard in the bathroom.'

'I see.'

'There's no other possible explanation because someone like you would never see anything in someone like me.'

Wouldn't he?

'I did warn you,' she added. 'And they do have a point.'

No, they didn't. 'What are you talking about?'

'The glowering, Theo.'

He frowned. 'The what?'

'You've been glowering at me all evening. I've been working my socks off and you just, well, *haven't*. Aren't you supposed to at least be *pretending* you're interested in me?'

Pretending was the trouble, he thought grimly. He was *too* interested. If he smiled at her, if he touched her anywhere other than the elbow, he might not be able to stop and, quite apart from the unacceptable lack of control that would incur, he would *not* breach her no kissing, no contact rule.

'If you're not going to meet me at least half-way,' she continued, 'you could do the decent thing and release me from this deal. There has to be another way. You could just let me go.'

There wasn't another way. And let her go? For

myriad reasons he didn't care to analyse, that was not an option. But neither was this state of affairs because, despite her attempts to brush off what she'd heard in the bathroom, it had clearly upset her and he wasn't having that.

'I have a better idea,' he muttered, taking her elbow again, wheeling her around and marching her back into the ballroom before she could protest. He came to a halt in the middle of the room, amidst the well-heeled, well-oiled guests milling about, and let her go. 'Where are they?'

'Where are who?'

'The women you overheard.'

'Oh.'

With a slight frown of concentration Kate scanned the room while Theo felt his displeasure rapidly morphing into anger.

'The woman in purple sitting over there,' she said after a moment, nodding in the direction of a table in the far corner, 'and the woman in red next to her.'

He knew both and he'd have expected better. Too bad. He strode across the room and stopped at table twelve. 'Samantha,' he said icily, looking down at the owner of the PR company he used.

'Theo,' Samantha simpered while batting her eyelashes up at him. 'So lovely to see you out. I was wondering if we might get together at some point to discuss—'

'The Knox Group no longer requires your services.'

In the moment of silence that followed, Samantha's eyes widened and her smile faltered. 'I'm sorry,' she said, giving her head a quick shake as if she'd misheard. 'What did you say?'

'Your contract expires at the end of the month,' he continued icily. 'It will not be renewed.'

'Oh, but—' she spluttered, turning pink. 'I mean... You can't do that.'

'I can.' He snapped his gaze to the brunette in the red dress who was sitting open-mouthed beside her. 'And you—Rebecca, isn't it? Stand down as chair or I'll find another charity to support.'

'Wh-what?' managed Rebecca, who, now he thought about it, was about as effective in her role as a wet dishcloth.

'You heard,' he said brutally. 'Do it. By nine a.m. tomorrow. And the next time either of you feels like gossiping about my fiancée, don't.'

If only Theo hadn't leapt to her defence like that, thought Kate, tossing and turning in bed that night as the memory of it circled around in her head and an unwelcome, unshakeable fuzzy warmth enveloped her.

She couldn't remember the last time someone had stood up for her, and the way he'd gone about it... The energy that had suddenly poured off him, the take-no-prisoners attitude of his and the sense of protectiveness... It was dangerously attractive and all too appealing to a certain someone who was starved of attention and achingly lonely. So appealing, in fact, that when they'd pulled up outside her building after a tautly silent journey, she'd inexplicably found herself wanting to ask him in for coffee, and maybe even more than that, which would have been unwise to say the least.

The trouble was, what he'd done made him so much harder to hate, and she needed to hate him because if she didn't, she could well end up liking him, and then where would she be? At the top of a very slippery slope that plummeted from the dizzying heights of excitement and hope to the miserable depths of disappointment and heartbreak, that was where.

But she had no intention of venturing anywhere near that slide so she could not allow his brief moment of chivalry detract from the rest of his lousy personality. She had to focus on the blackmail and the ruthlessness and not the feel of his hand on her elbow that burned her like a brand and the mesmerising eyes, dark with seething outrage and grim determination on her behalf.

She also had to accept that realistically there'd be many more naysayers like Samantha and Rebecca out there. Who knew what the press would make of the engagement? Of her? And then there were her colleagues. Her sister. How were they going to react?

She had no idea about any of it, but one thing was certain. If she had any hope at all of surviving the next few weeks, with whatever Theo or circumstances threw at her, ice-cool control and steely self-possession were the way to do it.

By lunchtime the following day, Theo had fielded more messages of congratulations than his limited patience could take, and the anger that had led to the instant dismissal of two significant business partners had swelled to fury.

How dared they? was the thought that kept ricocheting around his head during the three meetings he'd already held and wouldn't go away. How dared *anyone* attack what was his? Even temporarily his. So far the press had reported the facts without opinion, but if he ever heard *anything* in the way of sly accusation and measly insinuation again more heads would roll. Big heads. The biggest there were, in fact.

That he hadn't exactly behaved in an exemplary fashion himself was not on his conscience. Coercing Kate into a fake engagement by firing threats at her wasn't the most ruthless thing he'd done in pursuit of a goal, and what was at stake outweighed everything else.

What *did* trouble his conscience, however, was that she'd been right about his lack of input last night. He could have done better at playing the besotted lover despite having zero experience in the field, and if he hadn't been so wrapped up in frustration, he would have. It infuriated him now that he'd allowed himself to get so distracted, to lose sight of what was important.

However, it wasn't too late to rectify the situation. News of their engagement was out and in need of consolidation and that was precisely what he was going to do. In fact, he'd already taken steps, and by the time he was done no one would have any doubt whatsoever about its veracity.

Picking up the phone, Theo dialled the extension for the accounts department. 'Put me through to Kate Cassidy,' he snapped when his call was answered.

'I'm sorry, sir, she no longer works here.'

He scowled. What the hell? 'Why not?'

'She resigned this morning and was put on immediate gardening leave.'

'Where did she go?'

'Home, I believe, sir.'

'Thank you.'

Theo hung up, grabbed his keys, wallet, phone and the box he'd picked up this morning, and stalked out. As the lift whizzed him down to the garage he rang her mobile but the call went straight to voicemail. He left a curt message and got in his car, irritation pummelling through him as he negotiated his way through heavy London traffic. Without warning, Kate had gone off script and he didn't like it. Unpredictability led to confusion, which led to chaos, and he was not having his plans derailed by anyone or anything.

Half an hour later, he parked outside Kate's building, leapt up the five steps to her front door and pressed the buzzer for her flat.

'Hello?' came the tinny response an exasperating thirty seconds later.

'Kate, it's Theo. Let me in.'

There was a moment's silence and he thought

grimly that she'd better not be deliberately keeping him waiting as she had done last night, because this afternoon he was in no mood for games.

'First floor on the right,' she said eventually and he let out the breath he hadn't even realised he'd been holding.

The door clicked and in he went. He took the stairs two at a time and swung to the right and there she was, standing in the doorway to her flat, still in her work clothes although barefoot. Was she pleased to see him? Surprised? Annoyed? He couldn't tell. Her expression was giving him nothing, which was fine because what she thought of him turning up like this was of zero importance. He just wanted her back in line.

'What are you doing here?' she asked coolly, as if totally unaware of the disruption she'd caused.

'What are *you* doing here?' he countered.

'I resigned.'

'I heard.'

She raised her eyebrows. 'So?'

'May I come in?'

She frowned for a second, as if debating whether to let him into her space, and then shrugged, as if it didn't matter either way. 'Sure,' she said, turning her back on him and padding into her flat.

Ignoring the inexplicable irritation he felt at her indifference, he followed, automatically assessing the space as he did so. Bathroom on the left. Two bedrooms on the right. Compact open-plan kitchen, dining, living room at the end, flooded with light that poured in through two huge sash windows.

'Nice place,' he muttered. But on the small side. How was that going to work when the baby came along? he wondered before reminding himself sharply that it was none of his business and he couldn't care less.

'Thanks.' She walked into the kitchen and shot him a glance over her shoulder. 'Tea?'

'No.'

'So what do you want, Theo?' she asked as she filled the kettle with water and switched it on.

'I want to know why you resigned.'

'My situation was…untenable.'

Damn, he knew it. He flexed his hands. 'What did they say?'

'What did who say?'

'Anyone. Give me names.'

'No one said anything. It just felt awkward what with you and me and—' she waved a hand in the direction of her abdomen '—this. You own the company. Beyond congratulations, my colleagues didn't know what to say. And in all honesty I couldn't see it getting easier. So I resigned.'

His jaw clenched. 'I see,' he said, dismissing the jab at his conscience when the sacrifices she was having to make because of him inconveniently struck. 'Do you want another job?'

'At some point.'

'I have contacts. If you want one, you'll have one.'

'Thank you,' she said with a chilly smile that didn't reach her eyes. 'But so do I.'

Of course she did, he thought as the kettle pinged and she poured the water into a mug and stirred it. She didn't need his help. But she'd have it anyway. 'Whatever decision you choose to make,' he said, 'I will ensure that you're financially secure. Both of you.' That much he could do. 'I'll set up a fund.'

'That won't be necessary.'

Too bad. 'Nevertheless, it'll be there.'

'But you won't.'

'No.'

'Just out of curiosity, why not?'

Well, *that* was a question he wasn't going to

answer with the truth. 'There is no space in my life for a child,' he said, instantly crushing the brief, sudden surge of denial.

'You could make some.'

'No. I couldn't.'

'That's a shame.'

Not a shame. A necessity. 'That's reality.'

'Right,' she said, taking a sip of tea and setting the mug back down on the counter. 'So was there anything else?'

'There was one more thing.' He dug around in his pocket and pulled out the small blue velvet box he'd brought with him. 'This should help dispel any doubts people may have about us.'

For a moment she just looked at the box in silence. And then she stepped towards him and took it from him, her fingers brushing his and her proximity doing odd things to his equilibrium.

When she opened it, her eyes went wide and she let out a soft gasp that would have instantly transported him back to that evening in his office if he let it. 'Wow.'

'Do you like it?'

'Who wouldn't? Is it real?'

'Yes.'

She frowned. 'Borrowed?'

'No.'

'It's too much,' she said with a faint shake of her head as she closed the box and handed it back.

Theo felt the faint sting of something undefinable and ignored it. 'Just wear it,' he said sharply. 'It's important. For the narrative.'

'Okay, fine,' she said with a careless shrug that somehow stung even more. 'But only when we're out together.'

'I don't mind what you do when you're on your own,' he said. 'As long as you remember your role when we're out in public.'

'I'm unlikely to forget with this on my finger.'

As was he. Which was, after all, the point. 'And speaking of which,' he said, dismissing as ridiculous the inexplicable urge to demand she put it on now, 'tomorrow night we're going to the opening of a new wing at the National Gallery that my company has funded. And this time, Kate, don't keep me waiting.'

A fortnight later, Kate eased off her shoes after yet another function, and with a grateful sigh flopped onto her bed.

To call the last two weeks a whirlwind of activity was an understatement. She'd attended eight events, one antenatal appointment and a hospital scan. She'd been to see her sister to explain the engagement and the pregnancy as best she could without going into detail, and had been relieved when Milly had accepted without question that she was going to be an aunt. In fact, her sister had been delighted, had immediately announced that she was going to take up knitting. Their WhatsApp chat channel was now filled with pictures of tiny bootees, hats and cardigans in various stages of progress and Kate's heart squeezed at every one.

She'd also been getting used to not going into work. Being at home on a weekday felt very odd; however, she hadn't really had any option. Once the news of her engagement had broken, her astonished colleagues had initially swooned but then backed off, as if any office gossip might reach Theo's ears at which point they could all well be fired. She'd come to the swift conclusion that things would only get worse and had promptly handed in her notice, after which her entire floor had seemed to breathe a sigh of relief.

What she'd do about work in the future she had no idea. Discriminatory or not, she couldn't see a prospective employer jumping for joy about her condition. The hole in her bank account was still pretty big and any maternity benefit she might receive would hardly fill it. But she'd figure something out, maybe by reigniting the freelance bookkeeping she'd started, because she had no intention of ever touching Theo's money.

That he was going to set up a fund as he'd promised she had no doubt. Not so long ago he'd told her that there was barely a problem that couldn't be solved by throwing money at it and he clearly considered both her and their baby just such a problem.

As she sat up, it struck Kate once again that the way Theo had no interest in their child was strange. Weren't men, especially the alpha males among them, pre-programmed to instantly claim possession of their offspring, as a sign of their supremacy or virility or continuation of the bloodline or something? Wasn't it in some way evolutionary?

Well, Theo was as alpha and male as they came, yet he appeared to buck the trend. It was as if he was determined to distance himself from the very idea of it, and she couldn't help wondering why. Was it simply inconvenient? An obstacle en route to global domination? Was he really just too busy? Or did he genuinely not want a baby? She remembered thinking at one point, when she'd first delivered the news, that she'd caught a glimpse of pure terror in his eyes, but she must have been mistaken because she'd never met anyone less afraid of anything, so what was it?

However much it intrigued her, she could hardly ask. She'd already tried once, the afternoon he'd pitched up at her flat and filled her space with his dominating, disturbing presence, and had been firmly shut down. He didn't do personal and he didn't share anything other than the most superficial of information. The conversations they'd had over the last fortnight through necessity had been desultory at best, and, really, she didn't need to know.

To her surprise, though, he *had* taken on board her comments about his lack of participation when it came to faking their engagement. At the events they'd recently attended, he'd left no one in any doubt about his supposed intentions towards her. He no longer glowered in her direction. He even managed the occasional smile that flipped her stomach every time he bestowed it on her. He focused wholly on her, which was heady stuff, and ensured the ring he'd given her did not go unnoticed. And even though she knew it was all for show, that she shouldn't feel a million dollars when she was with him, her poor battered self-esteem lapped it up.

But she had to remember that this whole thing was nothing more than an elaborate charade, that the attention Theo paid her wasn't real, she told herself for the billionth time as she levered herself off the bed and unzipped her dress. He continued to show no remorse, no regret for the way he'd blackmailed her, and she couldn't fall again into the trap of crediting him with traits he didn't have. She had to stop drifting off into daydreams where every touch, every smile, was real. And she had to stop secretly putting the ring on at home, turning her hand this way and that so the beautiful stone caught the light and cast dancing sparkles on her walls, and pretending she had a man who loved her. The wave of longing she felt every time she succumbed to temptation did her no good at all.

Oh, how she wished she'd insisted on a time limit. There'd still been no word for Daniel Bridgeman and she didn't know how much longer she could keep it up. The pressure was immense. The battle between her head and her body was exhausting. And what was taking so long anyway? Their appearances in public had been noted, although thankfully with considerably less vitriol than experience had warned her to fear, and their performance had been entirely credible.

What if Mr Bridgeman had no intention of ever signing? Would she be locked into this absurd charade until Theo decided to release her? How would she bear it? She should never have agreed to it in the first place. She should have been tougher. She should have called his bluff and—

Her phone buzzed and she turned from the wardrobe where she was hanging the dress to reach down to fish it out of the evening bag that lay on the bed.

A message flashed up on the screen. From Theo.

Where was she to be paraded next? A charity ball? Business drinks?

No.

Italy, according to the text. On Friday. For the weekend. Because Daniel Bridgeman had finally, at long flipping last, been in touch.

CHAPTER NINE

'I CAN SEE why you like to travel by private jet,' said Kate, yanking Theo's attention from the document he'd been perusing for the past ten minutes with zero idea of its contents. 'I haven't bashed my knees once. It's heavenly.'

No, he thought grimly, watching her settle on the sofa as the plane climbed to thirty thousand feet and stretch her endless legs out. What was heavenly was the way she looked. And smelled. All the damn time.

Today she was wearing a pair of wide silky white trousers that clung to her legs whenever she moved and a blue top that matched her eyes. She looked fresh and lovely and she was immensely distracting. And even though he ought to be used to it after two weeks of outfit after incredible outfit and enforced proximity, he wasn't, because everything about her seemed to demand attention, whether she was with him or not, which was plain ridiculous.

His decision to give their fake engagement a

hundred per cent had undoubtedly been the right one, but that didn't mean it had been easy. Keeping Kate's no kissing, no inappropriate contact condition at the forefront of his mind had required more strength than he could have possibly imagined. Every time he touched her elbow or her back, he wound up wanting to touch a whole lot more and wondering how far he could go before it became unacceptable. And then there was the ring, blinding him at every opportunity it got. With hindsight he should have gone for something smaller but at the time, for some unfathomable reason, he'd wanted there to be no doubt whatsoever that she was his.

All in all, the last fortnight had been a more gruelling experience than he'd expected, and Daniel Bridgeman's invitation could not have come at a better time. Because while he had no intention of ever giving up on his goal, he'd found himself seriously considering his options on more than one occasion, which was disturbing in itself because once he'd embarked on a course of action he never doubted it.

'I'm delighted you approve,' he said, deciding he might as well give up on work and park the perplexing nature of his response to Kate in order to sit back and admire the view.

'It's hard not to. It's very comfortable.'

'How do you usually travel?'

'I don't much.'

Oh? 'I thought it was one of your hobbies.'

Her eyebrows rose. 'Why would you think that?'

'It was on your profile. Along with music and books.'

'Oh. Right. Yes,' she said after a pause. 'I'm surprised you remember.'

'I remember it all,' he said. 'The pictures in particular.'

She flushed and looked away. 'Ah. Yes. Those.'

'They seemed out of character.'

'I was desperate and had had three glasses of wine.' She gave a slight shrug. 'Not a strategy I can currently deploy, unfortunately.'

'Do you need to?' he asked, wondering for a moment whether she was as unsettled by him as he was by her and finding it an oddly pleasing thought.

'No, of course not,' she said dryly. 'What could possibly be stressful about being blackmailed into a fake engagement?' Which, to his mild disappointment, firmly dispelled *that* idea. 'Anyway, my real hobby is numbers.'

'Numbers?'

She nodded. 'That's partly why I became an accountant. Outside work, I love puzzles and brainteasers and things, and don't get me started on calculus. But I couldn't exactly put that in my profile. Numbers are hardly sexy.'

They were when she was talking about them. Her whole face lit up and her eyes sparkled. 'What do you like about numbers?' he asked with a baffling desire to expand the topic so he could see her light up some more.

'The reliability of them. They're black and white. They never let you down.' The look she shot him then was pointed. 'You know where you are with numbers.'

'Yet they're easy to manipulate.'

She arched an eyebrow. 'And you'd know all about manipulation, wouldn't you?'

He ruthlessly ignored the flaring of his conscience. 'I'm not going to apologise, Kate.'

'I'd be flabbergasted if you did,' she said. 'So what about you? How do you relax?'

'I don't.'

'Don't you have hobbies?'

'I don't have time.'

'All work and no play…'

'Are you suggesting I'm dull?'

She tilted her head and regarded him, her gaze

leaving trails of fire in its wake as it ran over him. 'Dull is not the word I would use to describe you.'

'Then what is?'

'Single-minded. Devious. Merciless. Cold. Calculating. Completely lacking in empathy. Oh, and mercenary.'

The adjectives tripping off her tongue so easily were entirely accurate, yet, oddly, her opinion of him stung. 'Please, don't hold back.'

'You did ask.'

And he wouldn't be making that mistake again. He didn't know why he had. Her assessment of him didn't matter. Her attitude, however, well, that *did*. 'We're going to be under scrutiny this weekend, Kate,' he said deliberately flatly. 'It's in everyone's interest to wrap the deal up as soon as possible, so I suggest you lose the prickliness.'

She levelled him a look and let out a sigh. 'Okay, fine,' she said with a shrug that made her silk shirt ripple enticingly over her chest. 'I can do that. I can play nice. Anything to expedite the goal.'

'Good.'

'So what happens when we land?'

'We drive to the Villa San Michele.'

'And then?'

'Tonight we're having dinner with the Bridgemans. Tomorrow there are meetings, and in the evening is their anniversary party.' Which he could definitely do without.

'Ah, yes. Fifty years,' she said with a trace of wistfulness he'd never understand in a million years. 'Can you imagine?'

No. He couldn't. He wouldn't. 'Unfortunately it can't be avoided.'

'Did you get them a present?'

'No.' He saw little to celebrate about marriage however long it lasted, quite frankly.

'Don't you think you should?'

'This whole weekend is purely about business. Gifts are not required.'

She looked at him for a moment, as if debating whether to push, but then, to his relief, said, 'It's your show,' and she was right. It was. Not that he had any intention of explaining himself to her. 'And on Sunday?'

'Bridgeman doesn't believe in working on Sundays.'

'Extraordinary.'

'Isn't it?' he said, responding to her faint smile with one of his own before he could prevent it. 'The final meetings will take place on Monday.'

'After which you'll know.'

'Precisely.'

'What's so special about this particular company?'

'It's up for sale.'

'But there must be hundreds of companies up for sale.'

'Not of this size.'

'What are you going to do with it if you get it?'

'*When* I get it,' he corrected, 'the majority of it will be absorbed into the Knox Group and the rest will continue to operate independently.'

'Isn't your company big enough already?'

'No,' he said bluntly. 'Not nearly.'

'What can you possibly have left to prove?'

'Everything.'

She seemed to have nothing to say to that but her eyes didn't leave his. They merely narrowed slightly, as if she were pondering some enormous conundrum, which for some reason made him feel as if he were sitting on knives.

'What?' he asked, irritated by the way his body was instinctively reacting to her scrutiny.

'I was just wondering how on earth you and my brother were ever friends.'

He froze, her words cutting right through his discomfort, obliterating the heat and filling him

with icy numbness. 'We weren't. We were acquaintances.'

'Oh? I got the impression you were friends.
But I guess acquaintances makes more sense.'

'In what way?'

'Well, you're not at all alike. I mean, Mike
was ambitious, sure, but you're on another level
entirely. He lacked your killer instinct. He had
lines. How on earth did you meet?'

'At the boxing club.'

She flashed him a sudden triumphant smile
and for a moment he forgot how to breathe. 'Aha!
So you *do* have a hobby.'

'I wouldn't call it a hobby,' he said, willing
his thundering pulse to slow. 'More a means of
keeping in shape.'

'Are you good at it?'

'Yes.' He'd had plenty of practice.

Her smile turned rueful. 'Mike wasn't.'

'No.'

'Did you box each other?'

'Only once.'

'Who won?'

'No one.'

'How come?'

'I collapsed.'

Her eyes widened. 'What happened?'

'I'd taken a blow to the ribs the week before. I hadn't given it any more thought but then when I was in the ring with Mike, my spleen ruptured. He got me to hospital. He saved my life.' Hence the debt that he should not have taken so long to pay back.

'I had no idea.'

'It wasn't something I wanted publicised.' The incident had rendered him weak, vulnerable, and had his competitors got wind of it they would have pounced within minutes.

'Are you all right now?'

'Yes.' Physically, at least.

'So what happened then?'

'Once I'd recovered we went for a drink. It became a regular thing.'

She nodded as if in understanding. 'An escape.'

'Yes. He was under a lot of stress.'

'I meant for you.'

'*I* have nothing to escape from,' he said, ruthlessly blotting out the great neon sign in his head that was flashing the word 'liar' at him.

Her eyebrows lifted. 'Not even work?'

'Not even that.'

'Hmm. So you knew what was going on with him?'

'Some of it.'

'Me, too.' Her cornflower-blue eyes filled with momentary sadness, and his chest tightened. 'I wish I'd known more, though. But he didn't once complain, not even when he had to leave university to come and look after me and Milly, *and* then find the money to move my sister when it became apparent she wasn't being looked after well.'

'What happened?'

'Nothing that awful. It was mainly little things. Cleanliness. The food. The size of the rooms. And then it became apparent that the staff— not exactly the warmest of people—were quick to medicate. Easier to manage the more unpredictable patients that way, I suppose. Fairview is about as different a place as it's possible to imagine. There's more space, outside as well as inside. The staff care. Milly moved just as soon as we could sort it. She's happy there, and well cared for.'

'She will have whatever she needs, Kate.'

'Thank you.' She paused. Then said with a sigh, 'I never appreciated the stress Mike must have been under. He worked day and night. We shared the day-to-day stuff, but financially he bore full responsibility. When he lost his job I wish he'd said something. He didn't have to carry the burden alone. I don't know how I didn't know, especially since he was living with me. I guess I didn't ask. He said he'd resigned to set up his own business and that he'd given up his flat to put the money into it and I just accepted it. But none of that was true.'

Theo frowned. 'No.'

'I feel so guilty.'

'If anyone is to feel guilty,' he said, unable to let her think she was in any way to blame and suddenly burning up with the need to confess and in some small way to atone for what he'd let happen, 'it's me.'

'Why?'

'His death was partly my fault.'

She stared at him in shock. 'What on earth are you talking about? He had an aneurysm. It was sitting there in his brain like a ticking time bomb. How could that possibly have been your fault?'

'I could have done more to help. To remove the stress. I should have insisted.'

'He had his pride. And he was stubborn.'

'That's no excuse.' And it wasn't because hadn't he already discovered what happened if he turned his back on someone who needed his help whether they wanted it or not? Hadn't his mother been enough? How many more people were to suffer before he learned? Whatever she chose to think he'd robbed Kate and her sister of their brother and he'd never forgive himself. 'I'm sorry.'

'There's really nothing to be sorry for,' she said. 'Truly. Did you know about the loans?'

'No.'

'Neither did I.'

'But I could have done,' he said bleakly. 'I should have done.'

'How?'

'A couple of weeks before he died, Mike mentioned he had something he wanted to discuss. I put him off.' He stopped and frowned, remembering how he'd instinctively kept the man at arm's length despite the huge debt he owed him. 'I regret that.'

'You came to the funeral.'

'It was the least I could do.'

She tilted her head, her gaze practically searing into his. 'Do you remember me suggesting a drink afterwards?'

He frowned. 'No.'

'You took it as a come-on.'

'Did I?'

'You did. And you said you weren't interested.

But it wasn't an invitation at all. I just wanted to chat to you about my brother.'

'I apologise,' he muttered, now recalling how Kate's grief had been too great for his guilt to handle and how in response he'd shut down, operating on automatic. 'It was a tough afternoon.'

'You're telling me.'

'How are you dealing with it?'

She bit her lip. 'I'm getting there. Most days I'm okay, but every now and then it hits me like a bolt from the blue. You'd think I'd be used to it by now. The grief, I mean. It's not as if I'm a stranger to it. I've lost more than most people do in a lifetime. Yet it still gets me right here.' She pressed her hand to her heart and rubbed. 'But there's nothing I can do about it. I can't change anything. So I have to just get on with it.' She tilted her head and regarded him thoughtfully. 'I do think, though, that if he'd lived, Mike would have been a good friend to you.'

The vice that had gripped Theo's chest in response to her suffering tightened. What could he say to that? He could hardly admit that he'd never have let things get that far. That the damage caused by his mother's rejection was irreversible and that the traces of it still affected the way he viewed every single person he met. 'Perhaps.'

'What are your other friends like?'

Non-existent. Which was fine with him. He didn't want or need friends. He was better off alone. Always. More importantly, other people were better off if things were that way. And this conversation was over.

'Quiet,' he said bluntly. 'Unobtrusive. They don't ask questions and they let me get on with my work.'

'Ah. Right,' she said with the flash of a grin that hit him square in the gut. 'Point taken. I'll leave you to it.'

They landed at Linate Airport mid-afternoon and the minute she stepped off the plane, Kate felt as if she could once again breathe, despite the thirty-degree heat.

How hard it had been to focus on her book when her attention kept wandering, her gaze drifting over to where Theo was sitting, head down, his brow furrowed in concentration as he worked at his laptop. How hard it had been not to think about the suite at the back of the plane with its enormous bed just begging to be rumpled. And then there'd been the urge to strike up the conversation again, which had been so insistent that her jaw ached with the effort of keeping her mouth shut.

Truth be told, she found Theo increasingly intriguing. Now she'd had an unexpected taste of conversation that went beyond pleasantries, she wanted more because she had the feeling there was a lot going on behind that cold, steely facade. She saw it in the occasional flicker in his eyes and the way his jaw sometimes tightened.

Despite her best intentions to remain aloof and keep his ruthlessness at the forefront of her mind like some sort of shield, she could feel her opinion of him beginning to soften. She might have called him cold and merciless and lacking in empathy, but that wasn't all he was. His misplaced guilt over Mike's death and the apology for his behaviour at the funeral had been genuine. Then there was that hint of humour when he'd effectively told her to shut up, which was all the more attractive because of its rarity. And now there was the car that was waiting for them on the tarmac, a gorgeous bright red convertible, low, sleek and powerful. Was it at all possible that he'd remembered what she'd once said about always wanting a nippy little convertible? What would it mean if he had?

Nothing sensible, she thought, if the warm fuzzy feeling spreading through her at the mere possibility was anything to go by. And certainly nothing that merited further analysis. She could not afford to let herself get distracted. She must not seek rainbows where there were none. She had to keep control of her wayward imagination and her precarious emotions and focus on the reality of her situation.

'Nice wheels,' she said, watching in admiration as Theo hefted their luggage into the boot as if it weighed nothing.

'It was all that was left,' he said and slammed the boot shut before striding round to the passenger door and opening it.

Oh. Right. Well, that cleared that up. Good. And frankly what did it matter how this car had ended up here? She still got to ride in it. So that annoying stab of disappointment could get lost.

'Lucky me,' she said with a bright, slightly forced smile as she walked towards him. 'No chauffeur?'

'I like to drive,' he said, unhooking his sunglasses from the v of his shirt and putting them on. 'Get in.'

* * *

By the time Theo pulled off the road an hour and a half later and drove through a pair of giant iron gates, Kate had come to a number of conclusions.

Firstly, the northern Italian countryside in summer was stunning. It had taken a while to get out of Milan, but once they'd left the suburbs there'd been nothing but lush greenery and an abundance of beautiful wild flowers. Secondly, there was something impossibly sexy about a gorgeous man driving a fast car in the sunshine, with his shirt sleeves rolled up to his elbows and sunglasses on. And thirdly, it turned out she had a thing for competence.

The way Theo handled the powerful car was nothing short of masterful. Unlike many of the other road users, he didn't drive recklessly. In the city he kept his cool when everyone else seemed to be yelling and gesticulating wildly, and on the open road that had brought them to the edge of Lake Como, he stuck more or less to the speed limit and didn't overtake on blind bends.

Safe. That was how she felt with him. Everything he did was calculated. Measured. He liked to be in control and he was careful. Maybe that was why he refused to engage with the pregnancy. Maybe it represented a careless moment that he was in denial about. Or maybe he really just didn't care.

Whatever.

It didn't matter.

She was probably overthinking things anyway.

What *did* matter and what she *ought* to be thinking about was that they were here, and it was time to slip into the role of adoring, snark-free fiancée, which thankfully had become easier with practice.

The long wide gravelled drive was lined with soaring cypress trees and the warm late afternoon air was filled with the sweet scent of jasmine and honeysuckle. When the drive split, Theo took the left fork, and a minute later pulled up outside a surprisingly modest house that was ochre in colour, had petrol-blue shutters at the windows and elaborate iron balconies, and exuded old soft warmth.

While Kate smoothed her windswept hair, Theo climbed out of the car and strode to the boot. 'It should be open,' he said. 'Go on in.'

'Can we?' Kate asked in surprise. 'Oughtn't we wait for our hosts?

'It's the guest house. It's all ours.'

Oh.

Oh, dear.

She hadn't anticipated she and Theo being on their own. In fact she hadn't given their accommodation any thought at all. But clearly she should have because this place didn't look big enough to have two bedrooms and what that might mean she didn't like to think.

In some trepidation, she pushed open the door and stepped inside, the sudden drop in temperature scattering goosebumps all over her skin. The flagstone floor was covered with a series of rugs in terracotta and white. The open-plan space was divided into cooking, dining and sitting zones. At the far end to her right was a huge fireplace. In front of it was a long, comfy-looking sofa and a table stacked with magazines. In the middle was a dining table that seated four, and on the left the kitchen. Off that was a utility room and a shower room, and then, up a wide flight of stone steps, the cool white en-suite bedroom.

Singular.

'Ah, Theo?' said Kate, heading back downstairs to where Theo was coming in with their bags and dumping them just inside the front door.

'What?'

'Bit of a problem…'

'What is it?'

'There's only one bedroom.'

His dark brows snapped together in a deep frown. 'Right.'

'I'm happy to take the sofa.'

'*I'll* take the sofa.'

'You're bigger than me.'

'You're pregnant.'

Ah, so he hadn't forgotten... 'Only just,' she said, not wanting to analyse the giddy pleasure and weird relief she felt at the knowledge.

'It's non-negotiable.'

It was ridiculous. 'We could share the bed.'

His jaw clenched. 'No.'

'We could put pillows down the middle or something.'

'No.'

'It *is* huge.'

'Kate,' said Theo tightly, fast running out of patience if his expression was anything to go by, 'the bed could be the size of Italy and it wouldn't be big enough if you were in it.'

Ooh, ouch.

His words landed on her with the sting of a thousand arrows and she had to fight hard to resist the temptation to curl in on herself. 'There's no need to be rude,' she said, feeling herself flush with mortification and searing disappointment that he thought of her like that.

'What?' he snapped, striding towards her and stopping a foot in front of her, his eyes suddenly blazing. 'No. I mean if we occupy the same bed, wherever you are in it, I will find you. And once I do, I can't guarantee there'll be no inappropriate touching.'

Oh.

Oh…

As his confession sank in Kate reeled, her breath catching in her throat and her head swimming. Was he really saying what she thought he was saying? Apparently he was. Which meant that, contrary to what she'd assumed, the attraction wasn't one-sided. He still wanted her. Intensely, judging by the hot, focused way he was looking at her.

Intriguing.

'I see,' she said huskily.

'Do you?' he said, his eyes dark and glinting. 'I'm not sure you do. But believe me, Kate, you do not want us sharing a bed.'

What if she did?

No. She didn't. She couldn't. Sex again with Theo, although no doubt explosive, would serve no purpose whatsoever. Besides, this whole situation was complicated enough and if she had any sense of self-preservation at all, she'd put it right out of her mind.

'Okay, fine,' she said, determined to stamp out the heat and desire pummelling through her and to regain control of her senses. 'Take the sofa.'

'Wise decision. Dinner's at eight.'

'And in the meantime?'

'You can do what you like,' he said, his expression now shuttered and inscrutable. 'I'm going for a swim.'

CHAPTER TEN

EARLIER, THEO HAD swum to the nearest prom-
ontory and back. It had taken him two hours
at full pace and it should have exhausted him.
It should have wiped out the ever-present lust
and the increasingly unbearable edginess. But it
hadn't. When Kate had emerged from the bedroom half an hour ago in a simple black shift
dress, her hair rippling around her shoulders like
a blonde wavy waterfall, all he wanted to do was
walk her back into the room, tumble her onto the
bed and to hell with dinner.

Of course there'd be only one bedroom in the
house. Everything about her, to do with her, was
designed to torment him, so the less than ideal
sleeping arrangements were par for the course.

What *wasn't* par for the course, what had had
him scything through the water as though a pair
of great whites were snapping at his feet, was
Kate's response to his declaration that he still
wanted her. He'd had no intention of telling her,
hell, he barely admitted it to himself, but when

she'd jumped to the wrong conclusion about why they would not be sharing a bed, she'd deflated right in front of him and he hadn't liked it.

She'd certainly perked up when he'd recklessly corrected her misconception. Her eyes had darkened to indigo and her breath had caught, and he had no doubt if she knew what she'd revealed she'd be appalled. He, on the other hand, had experienced a jolt of surprise, inexplicable relief that he wasn't alone in this and, unbelievably, even hotter, more desperate desire, which meant that this was going to be one very long weekend because while the attraction might be mutual there was no way he was going to do anything about it.

'Drink?'

With Herculean effort, Theo switched his gaze from where Kate was chatting to Elaine Bridgeman over by the window of the elegant drawing room to his host, the man he was here to see and to convince. 'Whisky,' he said, ruthlessly blocking out the sound of Kate's laughter and the threat to his peace of mind she presented as he accepted the drink. 'Thank you. And thank you for the invitation this weekend.'

'It was time,' said Daniel gruffly. 'I've been

following recent events with interest. Congratulations on your engagement.'

'Thank you.'

'Kate's very striking.'

'She is,' Theo agreed, resisting the monumental temptation to glance over at her.

'How long have you known her?'

'Not long. Seven weeks.'

'A whirlwind romance.'

Inwardly he recoiled, every cell of his body rejecting the idea, but outwardly he barely moved a muscle. 'Something like that,' he replied evenly.

'She used to work for you.'

'She did.'

'But she resigned recently.'

'Yes.'

'And you're okay with that?'

'Absolutely.'

'Has she got another position lined up?'

Theo felt a flicker of annoyance. He could hear the scepticism in Daniel's voice and he didn't like it one little bit. 'Not yet.'

'Pre-nup?'

'No.'

'Is that wise?'

It was irrelevant. Kate wasn't after his money. She wasn't after anything. Which was exactly how he wanted it. 'It's no one's business but mine.'

'Nevertheless—'

'Daniel.'

The older man looked at him shrewdly. 'Interesting. Well. Good. Glad to hear it. Very glad indeed,' he said, nodding and smiling as if he, Theo, had passed some sort of test. 'It may sound trite,' he added with a fond glance in the direction of his wife and sentimentality in his tone, 'but when you know, you know. I knew the second I laid eyes on Elaine that she was the one for me. We were married within eight weeks and I haven't regretted it for a second.'

It was a good thing Daniel didn't appear to expect a response to that because Theo didn't have one. What he did suddenly have was a churning gut, clammy skin and a thundering pulse, because whatever Daniel might be insinuating, Kate wasn't the one for him. She couldn't be. No one ever would be. She was a temporary fiancée, that was all. They barely knew each other. On Monday, with the deal in the bag, they'd go their separate ways. The all-consuming desire and the worrying sense of impending chaos would finally be gone and he couldn't be more looking forward to it.

'Have you set a date?' said Daniel, briefly yanking Theo out of the dark maelstrom of his thoughts.

'Not yet,' he said. Not ever.

'The pregnancy must be an added complication.'

The pregnancy wasn't anything except a means to an end. 'In some respects.'

'You're a lucky man.'

No, he wasn't. He wasn't lucky at all. Nor could he seem to get a grip. Because now not only did he feel as if he were about to pass out, but an image had slammed into his head, the image of a small child with his dark hair and Kate's blue eyes. No matter how hard he tried to wipe it out, the picture wouldn't budge, and suddenly his entire body prickled as if being stabbed with a hundred daggers.

Daniel continued to talk, but about what Theo had no idea. His host's words and his surroundings faded. His vision blurred. All he could see were the images that were whipping around his head, pushing aside everything else, making it pound and his heart race.

Why couldn't he block them out? he wondered, holding himself still through sheer force of will while inside he felt as if he were falling apart.

He'd done so successfully so far. He'd hardly noticed the way Kate kept touching and stroking her abdomen. He'd got more than used to the ring blinking at him and tormenting him by making him wish for things he had no right to wish for and could never have. So what was different about tonight?

The pressure. That was what it had to be. Immense and crushing, it was bearing down on him like a thousand-ton weight and exposing hairline cracks in his armour. This weekend was the most important of his life. He couldn't afford any mistakes. Nor could he afford weakness. Ever. He had to plaster over those cracks and bury that weakness. Now. For good.

'Are you all right, Theo?' he heard Daniel ask as, with superhuman effort, he cleared his head of the images, the sense of suffocation and chaos, and refocused his attention.

'Couldn't be better,' he replied smoothly, savagely dismissing the fear that it was a lie.

'Then let's go through to dinner, shall we?'

To hell with playing nice, thought Kate grimly, passing by Theo as he held open the villa's front door after what had to be one of the most excruciating, most stressful evenings of her life.

What was wrong with him?

He'd been tense ever since he'd returned from his marathon swim, the progress of which she'd surreptitiously watched from the bedroom window while admiring the way he powered through the water, but tension was nothing new. It seemed to be embedded in his DNA.

However, the moment they'd gone through to supper, she'd noticed a dramatic change in his demeanour. He'd been even more on edge than usual, his mood black and rippling with swirling undercurrents that luckily it appeared only she had been able to detect. Outwardly he'd engaged, but inwardly he'd been somewhere else entirely and she'd lost count of the number of times she'd had to cover for him. He'd ruined for her a delicious dinner on a terrace that had the most incredible views with interesting and gracious hosts, and she badly wanted to know why.

'Okay,' she said, turning round to face him and crossing her arms over her chest as he closed the door and locked it. 'What's wrong?'

'Nothing's wrong,' he said flatly.

'Was it something I said? Something I did?'

'You were fine,' he muttered, moving round her and fixed himself a drink from the kitchenette. 'Want anything?'

'A glass of water, please.'

He filled a glass with some water and thrust it at her. As she took it from him, their fingers brushed and electricity arced through her, setting fire to her blood and charging the air surrounding them with a crackling sizzle.

'Thank you,' she said, firmly banking down the heat, ignoring the sizzle and getting a grip.

'You're welcome.'

'Well, *something* was up,' she continued, not planning to let it go any time soon despite his reluctance to share because she was done with guesswork and assumption and always getting it wrong. 'You were all right at drinks and then not all right at supper. What happened in between?'

'Nothing happened.'

Right. 'Is there anything you want to talk about?'

His mouth twisted and he took a slug of his drink. 'No.'

'Sure?'

His jaw tightened. 'Leave it, Kate.'

'Because if there's something I can do to help…?'

'Okay, fine,' he snapped, slamming his glass down and shoving his hands through his hair. 'Actually, you *are* what's wrong.'

Oh. That was a blow. 'But I thought you said I did all right,' she said, frowning.

'You did,' he said, stalking towards her with a look in his eye that had her instinctively wanting to retreat. 'Do you want to know what I was thinking at dinner when I should have been paying attention to the conversation?'

Did she? Suddenly she wasn't at all sure. Every drop of intelligence she possessed was telling her that if she had any sense of self-preservation at all she should get far, far away because she sensed he was on the brink of a confession from which there'd be no return. But she'd pushed for this and she wasn't going to back down now, so she ignored the warning voice in her head, and said, 'Of course.'

'I was thinking about you, Kate,' he said, his voice low and rough as he came to a stop just in front of her. 'In that bed upstairs. With me. And no pillows down the middle.'

His eyes blazed into hers with more heat than she could possibly have imagined and her body flamed in response. Her pulse galloped and desire pooled between her legs. 'Well, *that's* not going to happen,' she said a lot more breathlessly than she'd have liked. 'Let's not forget the only reason I'm here, Theo. Because you blackmailed me. I wouldn't sleep with you again if you were the last man on earth.'

'Wouldn't you?'

'No.'

His dark eyes glittered. 'Are you sure about that?'

'I've never been surer of anything.'

'I could prove you wrong.' His gaze dropped to her mouth and her breath caught in her throat. 'Easily.'

And now she did take a step back. 'I would advise against it,' she said with a tiny jut of her chin, even though every inch of her was demanding he get on with it. 'Anyway, I don't believe you.'

His gaze snapped back up, a deep scowl creasing his brow. 'What, exactly, don't you believe?'

'You wouldn't let a little thing like desire get in the way of this deal.'

'It's hardly little.'

'You know what I mean,' she said, refusing to get distracted by thoughts of what exactly he might be referring to. 'This is nothing more than a diversionary tactic. Something else was bothering you. I know it. I know you.'

As if she'd dumped a bucket of cold water over his head, the heat left his gaze and his expression turned stony and forbidding. A chill ran through her and she shivered.

'You know nothing, Kate,' he said icily, 'and you most certainly don't know me.'

'Then talk to me.'

'There's nothing to talk about.'

And quite suddenly Kate had had enough. If Theo couldn't see that this weekend would go a whole lot better if they worked as a team then that was his lookout. What did it matter if he didn't want to tell her what troubled him? They were nothing. She didn't need to know. In fact, it was probably better that she didn't know, because the last thing she wanted was to develop sympathy for him. Or *any* kind of feelings, for that matter.

'Okay, fine,' she said with a shrug as a wave of weariness washed over her. 'It's late. I'm tired. And I give up. Have it your own way. I don't care any more than you care about the fact that I've given up my weekend for this and for you and am therefore missing a visit to my sister for the first time in years. But you really ought to rethink your attitude, because I might have been able to cover for you tonight but I can't keep doing it, and Daniel Bridgeman is no fool.'

Annoyed by the inexplicable disappointment

rushing through her and now just wanting to be anywhere he wasn't, Kate turned on her heel to head up the stairs. But as she did so the glass flew from her fingers and smashed into the wall, sending water flying before shattering into a thousand tiny pieces.

For a second she simply stood there staring at the broken glass lying on the floor, the echo of the crash bouncing off the walls, and then she snapped to. 'Terrific,' she muttered beneath her breath, stalking to the kitchen and yanking open cupboards in search of a dustpan and brush. Pregnancy induced clumsiness. Just what she needed.

But as she marched back and began to sweep up the glass, she caught a glimpse of Theo out of the corner of her eye, and something about what she saw made her stop. Straighten. And abandon the clearing up. Because he was utterly rigid. White. A bead of sweat was trickling down his temple and he didn't appear to even notice.

'Theo?' she asked in alarm, her frustration with him suddenly history. 'Are you all right?'

But he didn't answer. He didn't move a muscle. He seemed completely lost in his own world, and for some reason her heart squeezed. Before she could consider the wisdom of it and spurred on by an instinct she didn't understand, she walked over to him, avoiding the remains of the shattered glass, and lifted her hand to touch his face.

And then he reacted.

With lightning-like reflexes he grabbed her wrist and held it. Kate let out a startled gasp and for the briefest of moments they, time, everything, froze. She could hear nothing but the thundering of her heart, could see nothing but his eyes, which burned with myriad emotions she couldn't begin to identify.

And then a split second later the shutters slammed down and he let her go as if scalded and now it was her turn to remain rooted to the spot. She slowly lowered her arm and absently rubbed her wrist, but her entire body trembled and her mind reeled with the sickening suspicion that Theo's reaction had been the instinctive response of someone anticipating a blow. Expecting it. And the unexpected tumult of emotion that rushed through her at the thought stole her breath.

'So. Nothing to talk about, huh?' she said quietly when she could finally speak, her heart hammering and her entire body filling with a sudden and inexplicable burning rage towards whoever was responsible for it.

'Go to bed, Kate.'

* * *

As he watched Kate head slowly up the stairs and then disappear into the bedroom, the door closing behind her with a quiet click, Theo felt the icy numbness fade and into its place stormed such revulsion, horror and repugnance that his knees nearly gave way. The room spun around him and he couldn't breathe.

He'd grabbed her wrist, was the thought hammering around his head as his pulse pounded and his gut churned. Not tightly. But definitely firmly. He'd acted on instinct. He'd lost control. Not once in the years since he'd walked out of the squalid flat he'd grown up in had it happened. There'd been triggers, the occasional flash of memory, but he'd handled them. However, not so just now, and if he'd ever doubted the wisdom of his decision to stay away from Kate and the child that doubt was gone for ever. A better man would send her home.

What could she possibly think of what had happened? She had to be horrified. Maybe even terrified of what he might be capable of. At the very least she had to have questions. And since he wasn't a better man and he wasn't going to send her home, he had to give her the answers. He had no option. Despite every cell of his body rejecting the idea, he owed her an explanation. She had a right to know about the genes he carried and he couldn't have her looking at him with apprehension and uncertainty for the next forty-eight hours. He needed to clear the air. He needed to give her reassurance. Now.

Setting his jaw and galvanising into action while his brain shut down everything but the cold bare facts, Theo took the steps two at a time and banged on the door. 'Kate?'

'Come in.'

Bracing himself, although for what he had no idea, he opened the door and went in. Kate was sitting on the edge of the bed, her face pale and her eyes troubled.

'Are you all right?' he said grimly, scouring her expression for signs of pain and fear. He saw none, but he well knew that that didn't mean they weren't there.

'I'm fine.'

'Did I hurt you?'

'No.'

'Are you sure?'

'Yes.'

'Let me look.'

With a tiny sigh, Kate held out her arm and he stalked over to her, taking the wrist he'd grasped and examining it for marks, which thankfully didn't exist.

'You see,' she said softly. 'It's fine.'

He let her go and stepped back, shoving his hands through his hair. 'It's not fine.'

'Really.'

'I owe you an explanation.'

'No, you don't,' she said with a quick shake of her head. 'If anyone owes anyone anything, I owe you an apology.'

Theo frowned. 'What for?'

'Pushing. I had no right.'

'You had every right.' Because she'd been bang on when she'd confronted him on his attitude over dinner. Despite his conviction he'd dealt with it, he hadn't been able to shake the image of that child, and the realisation that his hold on his control wasn't as invincible as he'd assumed had been deeply disturbing and worryingly all-consuming.

'When you dropped the glass,' he said, addressing the part of the evening he understood marginally better and did need to explain, 'it triggered memories. Bad ones.'

She swallowed hard and lifted her shimmering gaze to his. 'Of abuse?'

He ruthlessly ignored those memories clamouring to be let out of the cupboard he kept them locked in and nodded once. 'Yes.'

Her eyes seemed to suddenly blaze. 'Who?'

'My father,' he said, totally in control, his voice utterly devoid of emotion as he relayed the facts. 'I grew up on the roughest estate in west London. We had virtually no money. Dad lost his job as a builder when he fell off a ladder on a construction site just after I was born. He never worked again. My mother was a cleaner. What little she brought in he drank, along with most of the benefits. When he'd had too much he threw things. Plates. Cups. Glasses. Anything he could lay his hands on. And when he'd run out of things to smash he took his frustrations out mainly on her, sometimes on me. Punches and kicks were his speciality.'

For a moment Kate didn't say anything, and Theo could understand her silence. What he'd just told her, the implications of it, was a lot to process. 'Did anyone know?' she asked eventually, her voice oddly gruff.

'No.'

'*Does* anyone know?'

'No.'

'What happened to him?'

'He died,' he said bluntly. 'Five years ago.' As

the next of kin, he'd received the call. When he'd heard the news he'd felt nothing.

'And your mother?'

'She had a brain haemorrhage three years before that. Caused by him, I suspect, but the evidence was inconclusive.'

'She stayed with him?'

'Yes.'

'Why?'

His chest tightened for the briefest of moments and memory and emotion flared before he got a grip and shut both down. 'I don't know. Initially I assumed it was because she had no means of escape or subsequent support.' But it hadn't been because she'd refused every one of the many offers he'd made.

'Is your early business success any coincidence?'

'No.'

'You made a lot of money fast.'

'By the time I was sixteen I'd amassed enough to support us both. I had it all set up.'

'What happened?'

'She refused to come with me. She didn't want to leave him.'

She stared at him in growing disbelief. 'So you left on your own?'

'Yes,' he said bluntly, as a familiar dull stab of guilt hit him in the chest. 'I realise I should have stayed.'

'No. I don't mean that,' she said, suddenly so fierce that it sent a shaft of warmth burning through the ice inside him. 'I mean, how could she not have gone with you?'

'I don't know,' he said unflinchingly since he'd learned to live with the fact that that was a question to which he would never know the answer a long time ago.

'I can't imagine what your childhood must have been like,' she said, her eyes filling with compassion that he neither wanted nor needed.

'I wouldn't ever want you to,' he said. 'I wouldn't want anyone to.'

She went very still. 'Is there any reason why they should?'

'Abuse engenders abuse.'

She stared at him, growing paler, other emotions that he couldn't begin to identify mingling with the compassion. 'Not necessarily.'

'The chances are high.'

'But not inevitable, surely.'

'It's a risk I will never be willing to take.'

'But—'

'No, Kate,' he interrupted, holding up a hand.

'Don't. I don't want to discuss it. I just wanted to explain what happened earlier. And to reassure you that you are in no danger from me. You have nothing to fear. I will make sure of that. There is no need to refer to the subject again. It needn't affect anything. It mustn't. I'll see you in the morning. Goodnight.'

Needn't affect anything? Kate thought, watching Theo walk out and close the door behind him while she tried to process everything he'd just revealed. How could he possibly think that? How could he think *any* of it? Most of all, how could he *ever* believe that she had something to fear from him? She'd experienced many, *many* emotions since she'd met him, but fear hadn't been one of them and never would be.

What he'd told her *did* affect things. Hugely. If he laboured under the heartbreaking impression that he might somehow be capable of harming her and the baby, it was no wonder he'd displayed such a lack of interest in and engagement with her pregnancy. And it certainly threw light on his fierce drive to succeed.

How had he ever got over his mother's rejection? she wondered, her throat tight and her eyes stinging as she struggled to process everything he'd said. Perhaps he hadn't. Did anyone? She'd learned to live without her mother, but her mother hadn't had a choice. His had, and she'd abandoned him. He'd had no siblings. He'd been all alone.

How tough and determined he had to have been in order to survive. How strong and resilient. It would hardly be surprising if that need for self-preservation was still deeply ingrained. She had first-hand experience of how old habits died hard. What had happened clearly continued to affect him. The way he'd presented her with the facts with such little emotion had spoken volumes, and it tugged on her heartstrings.

So where did she go from here? Should she try and make him see that history didn't have to repeat itself? That he posed no threat and that he could absolutely be a part of their child's life? Or should she leave well alone? On the one hand, she owed it to their child to at least try, but on the other, Theo had made it very clear that the subject was closed, and it was far too sensitive an issue for her to bulldoze her way through.

Whatever the options, now was not the time to subject him to her amateur psychology, she knew. This deal he was pursuing might well be wrapped up in his sense of self-worth and the need to prove something, and now she understood a bit more about why, there was nothing she would do to jeopardise it. So no matter how much she thought he needed to talk to someone about the trauma he'd suffered, no matter how much she wished she could help, all she could do was pretend that the last half an hour hadn't happened and carry on as if nothing had changed.

CHAPTER ELEVEN

THE TERRACE OF the Villa San Michele, the venue for the Bridgemans' golden wedding anniversary party, which was in full swing, had been spared no expense. Lights had been strung in and between the trees and around the railings. At one end, a buffet had been set up, the long wide trestle table laden with salads and cold meats and cheeses. A string quartet was playing something light and cheerful at the other, and in between a fountain tinkled with water that shimmered with gold dust. Earlier, boats sped across the lake that sparkled beneath the setting sun, delivering guests whose diamonds sparkled in the softening light and whose languages included English, Italian and who knew how many others. Now, champagne and conversation flowed and joy and sentimentality abounded.

It was absolutely the last place Theo wanted to be.

The noise was giving him a headache and the sense of suffocation that had dogged him all day was intensifying, tightening his collar and covering his skin in a cold sweat. He needed solitude. Time and space to deal with the fallout from last night. Because while he'd had no option but to share with Kate the basic details of his upbringing, he had the stomach-curdling feeling that by giving her a piece of himself he'd put into play something that couldn't be stopped. Look at the plan he'd made for the free day they had tomorrow, which served no practical purpose and was in no way necessary other than to assuage the guilt he felt about the sacrifice she'd had to make this weekend because of him, which should not have bothered him but did.

He had the feeling impending doom was hurtling towards him, and for the first time in over a decade he was in the petrifying position of facing a situation for which he had no strategy.

If only he could block Kate out the way he blocked out anything that threatened his peace of mind. It wasn't as if he hadn't tried. And it wasn't as if he hadn't had enough to focus on today with the intense all-day meetings he'd had with Daniel.

But he couldn't. She invaded his thoughts without warning and he seemed to be constantly tuned to her frequency. Such as earlier this evening when he'd been standing on the terrace of the guest house, looking out over the lake as he waited for her to emerge. He'd left the house at daybreak after a sleepless night and hadn't seen her since, and he'd been brooding about how she would now respond to him. Would she believe that she had nothing to fear from him? Or would she view him with doubt and suspicion?

His entire body had started prickling with awareness, alerting him to her presence behind him, and he'd experienced a rare moment of hesitation before turning. But her gaze had been clear and she'd been wearing a smile that had hit him in the solar plexus, and the relief that she seemed to be all right had been indescribable.

That awareness had not faded. At every second of every minute of the last couple of hours he'd instinctively known where Kate was when she wasn't with him. The magnetic pull of her was irresistible and he was finding it increasingly hard to stop himself clamping her to his side and keeping there.

The way she'd called him darling and wrapped her arm around his waist when they'd been talking to the Bridgemans earlier hadn't helped. Why had she done that? She hadn't before. Didn't she know how close to the edge of losing it he was?

How sick and tired he was of fighting the desire he felt for her? How much he wanted another night, two, with her before they went their separate ways?

If she'd had any inkling how close this evening he'd been to grabbing her hand and hauling her back to the guest villa she'd have been shocked. She wouldn't be sipping champagne and laughing as she chatted with an ease he could only envy. She'd be making arrangements to leave just as soon as was humanly possible. And he'd be cheering her on. Because he didn't like the way she made him feel. He didn't like the desire and the need slithering around inside him, rushing through his blood, making a mockery of his reason and battering his defences.

He particularly didn't like the way the guy she was talking to was leaning towards her. Or looking at her, for that matter. As if he was dazzled. Had the man no respect? What the hell was he thinking? Kate was *his* fiancée. His.

And yet Theo couldn't blame him for wanting to get close. She was blinding. The gold silk dress she had on was tight, which emphasised her phenomenal curves, and strapless, which revealed an expanse of sun-kissed skin that he ached to touch. It was knee-length and split to the thigh on one side, which left her lovely long legs exposed, and as for the stilettos she was wearing, well, those had him thinking of her naked beneath him with the spikes digging into his back.

The confidence she exuded tonight surrounded her like some kind of aura. She was enjoying herself, holding herself tall, as if she didn't care any more about her height or what anyone thought of her. She was no longer afraid, he realised with a start. No longer ashamed. Was she aware of the seismic transformation she'd undergone? Did she know how mind-blowingly attractive she was?

He did.

And as she laughed at something the man she was talking to said, everything in Theo's head disappeared beneath a wave of such intense desire it nearly took out his knees. The concern about what Kate might think of him... The terrifying notion that his grip on his control was weakening and that everything he'd spent so long building was about to implode... It all slipped away until all he was left with was a primitive need to claim and possess. And while on one level he realised he was allowing desire to surge and swell to such an extent it overwhelmed more complicated matters, on another he simply no longer cared.

Oh, dear Lord, Theo was coming over.

Up until this point Kate thought she'd been doing really rather well. Although she'd been aware of his gaze on her all evening, burning her up, making her unable to properly follow any of the conversations she'd been having, she'd just about managed to keep her cool.

How, though, she had no idea. She was by no means firing on all cylinders. She hadn't slept well. She'd ached too hard for the boy Theo had been and the man he'd become. When she thought about what he must have suffered...well, she didn't know and she wanted to, so after a few fitful hours she'd fired up her laptop and re-searched it, which had been a mistake because what she read tore at her heart.

She'd barely registered him leave the villa at dawn—she'd been in too much of a state—but she'd spent the rest of the morning in limbo, the hours dragging while her mind raced. She'd swum and sunbathed, caught up on the news and replied to a few emails, and then had lunch with Mrs Bridgeman, but she hadn't been able to concentrate through any of it, not even her hostess's cross-questioning about how she and Theo had met and her enthusiastic interest in their non-existent wedding plans, which somehow she'd managed to muddle her way through.

She hadn't seen Theo until she'd found him waiting for her on the terrace of their villa earlier this evening. She'd noted the tension in the rigidity of his shoulders and the lines of his tall, powerful frame, and at that moment all she'd wanted to do was hug him. Comfort him. Which was absurd since he didn't need her or anyone and she was supposed to be pretending last night hadn't happened, but there it was.

And when he'd turned round, looking so darkly, smoulderingly handsome in his black dinner jacket and white shirt it had stolen her breath, it hadn't been simple desire that thumped her in the gut. It had been something deeper and more intense. Something that grabbed hold of her heart and squeezed and made her think of that slippery slope she'd been so wary of. The lines that defined their relationship were blurring, and if she wasn't very careful indeed she'd be careering headlong down it.

Assuming she wasn't already, of course.

Worryingly, the fact that Theo had blackmailed

her into this whole thing no longer seemed to matter quite as much as it once had. Those feelings she'd been so worried about had smashed through the flimsy dam of her resistance and were flowing through her, hot and fierce. And now he was striding towards her, his expression focused entirely on her, dark and forbidding, and her whole body was alive with anticipation. Shivers ran up and down her spine. Her pulse galloped. And she had the dizzying sinking feeling that she'd been waiting all evening for this moment, the moment he came to claim her.

With a murmured, 'Excuse me,' she moved away from the man she'd been talking to just as Theo came to a stop a foot in front of her. His eyes were dark and glittering with a hint of uncharacteristic wildness, and her mouth went dry.

'Dance with me,' he said, his voice so low and rough it was practically a growl.

Her pulse leapt, the tightly leashed hunger she could hear in his tone sending heat straight to her centre and detonating tiny explosions along her veins. 'I don't think that would be wise,' she murmured, swallowing hard and thinking that quite apart from anything else she never knew what to do with her arms and always worried she'd fall flat on her face.

His gaze darkened. 'I do.'

'Because it would look good?'

'No.'

'Then why?'

'Because I want to.'

Oh.

Well, so did she. Quite desperately. The sultry beat of the music that had replaced the string quartet was thudding through her body. The way he was looking at her was scrambling her senses. To hell with humiliating herself. She wanted to touch him in ways that were wholly inappropriate off the dance floor but entirely acceptable on it and the best thing was, he would never know.

'Then let's dance.'

Theo didn't need telling twice. He held out a hand and she took it and he led her onto the dance floor. And as he drew her into the circle of his arms, nothing at that moment seemed as important as his hands on her back, searing through the fabric of her dress and setting her on fire. Nor did anything seem as necessary as touching him. So she put her hands on his chest, the way his muscles tensed beneath her palms sending heat shooting through her, and slid them up and around his neck.

As they swayed in time to the music, she realised that the worst thing that could happen on a dance floor wasn't falling flat on her face. It was losing her mind. Because she couldn't help responding to the strength and hardness of his body and pressing closer. She couldn't help wishing they were alone so that she could get him naked and touch some more.

So what was to be done?

If the feral look in his eye and the thick, hard length pressing insistently against her were anything to go by he wanted her as much as she wanted him. But ever since that no kissing, no touching condition she'd hit him with he'd been careful about where and how he touched her, which meant that unfortunately it was unlikely he'd simply haul her off to have his wicked way with her.

Did she have the guts to suggest it herself? What would he think if she did? Yes, he obviously wanted her but she'd never met anyone with such control. What if she indicated she'd like a repeat of that evening in his office and he turned her down? Maybe she should steal a kiss, she thought dazedly, staring at his mouth and feeling her lips tingle. He wouldn't be able to reject that, not when they were in the possible presence of the person they were here to fool.

Fevered tension filled what little space there was between them, and the air sizzled and suddenly she couldn't bear it any longer. His mouth was mere centimetres from hers and all she could think about was how it would feel on hers and how desperate she was to find out.

Desire swept through her, drowning out reason and common sense until all that was left was instinct. Helpless to stop herself, she lifted her face and moved her head forward and touched her lips to his and it was dizzying until she realised he'd gone utterly rigid and was not responding and that headiness turned to excoriating mortification.

Flushing with a different kind of heat and feeling like an utter fool, Kate jerked away but she didn't get far because a split second later Theo had yanked her tight against him and crushed his mouth back to hers, kissing her with such heat and intensity that if he hadn't been holding her in his arms she'd have collapsed into a heap on the floor.

After what felt like hours, he broke the kiss, his breathing as ragged as hers, his eyes dark and his face tight with barely suppressed need. 'Enough,' he said roughly.

'Not nearly,' she breathed, staring at his mouth, longing to feel it back on hers.

'We're making a scene.'

'Isn't that the point?'

He tensed and when her gaze flew to his she thought she saw a rare flicker of uncertainty in his eyes. 'Is it?'

And she could lie and say yes, but she didn't want to and, besides, hadn't they gone beyond that? 'No.'

A muscle hammered in his jaw. 'Tell me what you want, Kate,' he said, and she instantly thought that the only answer to that was 'more' because she wanted another night. Possibly two. It wasn't as if she believed things would continue beyond that. She knew perfectly well that once this weekend was over, once the deal was signed, that would be that. But she didn't want to think about what lay ahead for her when she was home—unemployment, single parenthood, reality. She didn't want to think about what Theo had told her and how it made her feel about him. She wanted to lose herself in the heat and the passion that he unleashed in her and just for once live in the moment. 'I want us to go back to the villa,' she said, her heart thundering with anticipation and excitement. 'Together. Now.'

Flames leapt in his dark eyes and his hold on her tightened. 'You do know what will happen if we do, don't you?'

'Well, I know what I'm *hoping* will happen.'

'Then let's go.'

It took two minutes to say their thank-yous and goodbyes. Five to get to the guest villa. One to shove open the front door, hustle Kate in, close it and push her up against it.

For a moment Theo just stared at her, the moonlight flooding in through the window casting pale shadows across her face, losing himself in the depths of her eyes and not caring that she was able to see straight into his, into the empty black hole where his soul should be. With any luck she wouldn't see that. Instead she'd simply see the strength of his need for her and the relief that incredibly she was on the same page.

She was breathing hard. Her eyes were shining and she was shaking with what he hoped to God was excitement, and then she lifted her chin and arched an eyebrow as if asking what he was waiting for, and that was it.

As his control snapped he slammed his mouth down on hers and kissed her as if it had been months instead of minutes. Beneath the onslaught she moaned and opened her mouth and when his tongue met hers, desire instantly flared like a flame to touchpaper. She whipped her arms around his neck and tilted her pelvis to his and it was all the encouragement he needed.

He pulled her closer, devouring her mouth, her jaw, her neck. She pushed her hands beneath the lapels of his jacket, and, without breaking the kiss, he shrugged out of it. She clawed at his shirt, yanking it free while he found the zip of her dress and slid it down. He lifted the hem and she wiggled her hips, and a second later he'd peeled it up over her head and tossed it on the floor.

And then he put his hands to her waist and his mouth to her breast, and when she whimpered, he drew her hard pink nipple between his lips and she whimpered some more.

But it wasn't enough. It had been driving him mad not knowing what she tasted like, so he sank to his knees, and when she gasped and instinctively clamped her legs together, he slid a hand between her knees and eased it up. And when he reached the curls at the juncture of her thighs, he touched her there and stroked her lightly and she gave a soft sigh of surrender as her legs fell apart.

Unable to wait a moment longer, Theo tugged her knickers down and then off. He clamped his hands to her hips and put his mouth on her and then he knew exactly how she tasted. Sweet. Delicious. Irresistible. As he licked and sucked he felt her tremble and he held her more firmly, the desire rocketing through him almost unbearable.

Above him, there came a faint, 'Oh, God,' followed by the gentle thud of her head against the door, and he increased the pressure, the tempo, while she sobbed and gasped, and then her hands were clutching at his head while she pushed against him and then, with a soft hoarse cry, she shattered.

Tight with the need for release, he kissed his way back up her trembling body until he was upright again. Her eyes were glazed. Her cheeks were pink and he didn't think he'd ever seen anything so beautiful, or anyone so desperate, and something shifted in his chest, something that might have concerned him if the way she was grappling with the button and zip of his trousers hadn't concerned him more.

'Stop,' he grated, summoning up every drop of his control to still her hand.

'Why?'

'I don't have a condom,' he said tautly, every muscle of his body screaming in denial.

Devastation flitted across her face. 'What?' she said dazedly. 'No.'

'Yes.'

'It doesn't matter. It's too late. You can't get me more pregnant. And I trust you, Theo. On this. On everything.'

His chest tightened. 'You shouldn't. Not on everything.'

'I know. But I do.'

Then she was a fool. But she had a point about it being too late. He was granite hard and the need to be inside her was burning through him like wildfire. There was no going back from this. Wild horses wouldn't drag him away from her now. So he crushed his mouth to hers, lifted her leg to open her up to him and thrust into her tight wet heat and it was heaven.

He gave her a moment to accommodate him but he couldn't hold still for long. Beneath his ravenous kisses she moaned and clung onto his shoulders. He began to move, knowing it wasn't going to take much when she matched his every thrust with hot, increasingly frantic demands of her own.

And it didn't. Within moments she was clenching around him again, gasping his name and sobbing and digging her fingers into his shoulders, and that was it. He felt his orgasm building in strength and momentum, and then it was barrelling through him as, with a roar, he thrust fast and hard, burying himself as deep as he could before fiercely and never-endingly spilling into her.

CHAPTER TWELVE

BY THE TIME Kate had recovered from the shuddering effects of two spectacular orgasms, she noticed that, encouragingly, Theo had got himself naked.

'Bedroom,' he muttered, grabbing her hand, his eyes so dark with the promise of more to come that incredibly she wanted him all over again. 'Now.'

But the only thing holding her up was the door, and she had the helpless feeling that if she moved, she might well crumple to the floor. 'I can't,' she said huskily, finally able to run her gaze over him, which only weakened her limbs further. 'Legs. Like noodles.'

So he scooped her up and carried her, all six foot one of her, as if she weighed nothing, and strode up the stairs and into the bedroom. And while he was doing so, it suddenly struck her that she didn't feel self-conscious at all. Moments ago, she'd been upright, bare, and totally exposed to him, and after her initial reservation, she'd loved it. Now her bits were jiggling and she was all squashed up against him, which wasn't exactly flattering, and she didn't even care. In fact, she felt incredible. As if she could do anything. Dance without falling over. Wear heels without towering above the man beside her. Take on the world.

And suddenly she wanted to find out not only how far she'd come but how far she could go. So when Theo took her into the softly lit bedroom and set her down beside the enormous bed, she planted one hand on his chest and pushed.

He landed in the middle of it, and stared at her first in shock and then with a slow smile that robbed her of breath. He lifted himself up onto his elbows and arched an eyebrow, as if daring her to go through with whatever she was planning, and while she didn't have a plan she was more than up for accepting the challenge.

'Where should I start?' she asked, uncertainty nevertheless making her hesitate.

'Wherever you want.'

'What if you don't like it?'

His eyes gleamed. 'I suspect there is nothing you can do that I won't like, Kate.'

Okay, then.

Gathering her courage, she joined him on the

bed and let her gaze roam all over him. There was so much of him to explore, so she straddled him, the hard length of him pressing into her in the most delicious way, and ran her hands over his shoulders and then down his arms, feathering her fingertips over the dips and contours of his muscles and delighting in the way they tensed beneath her touch.

And now she wanted to taste him, so, remembering the pleasure she felt when he held her breast and teased her nipple, she bent down and touched her tongue to his and licked. He shuddered and hissed out a breath, so she did it again, the salty tang of his skin making her taste buds dance and sing, and suddenly she wanted to touch him and taste him everywhere. Thoroughly. The way she'd been too afraid to try all those weeks ago.

And though she'd never done anything remotely like it before, and though she was bound to be clumsy and inept, she'd never know if she didn't try. If he laughed she could always make him pay. Somehow.

Shifting herself lower, she ran a hand down his body, over the ridges of his muscled abdomen and the faint trace of a scar, and feeling him shudder. Tentatively she touched the head of his erection and then stroked her fingers along his rock-hard length. His skin there was surprisingly soft and velvety and she was gripped by the need to feel it properly, so she wrapped her hand round him and slid it gently up from base to tip and then down again.

Theo growled and thrust into her hand, which was intriguing. As was the bead of liquid gathered at the tip. She rubbed her thumb over it and his hips jerked. She bent her head and licked, and was about to do it again when he put a hand at the back of her head, his fingers tangling in her hair, and pulled her away.

'You need to stop,' he said, his breathing sketchy and harsh.

Her heart skipped a beat as her stomach plummeted. Oh. Had she been doing it wrong? 'Really?'

'If you don't, this will be over embarrassingly quickly.'

Phew. She hadn't been doing it wrong. And she didn't mind that he'd stopped her, because his rampant need for her and the tight desperation she could hear in his voice were sending shockwaves of desire pulsing through her and if she didn't get him inside her just as soon as she could she might well combust.

She kissed him because it had been too long since her lips had been on his, shifted again and pressed her pelvis into his. Acting on the need drumming away inside her she rubbed herself against him and it sent such sparks of pleasure through her that she did it again and again, until her head was spinning and she couldn't carry on kissing him because she couldn't breathe. She tore her mouth from his, her breath coming in short sharp pants, and all she could think about was racing towards a finishing line that was simultaneously rushing towards her.

'Kate,' he growled and she opened her eyes to see his brows drawn in concentration and his jaw clenched.

'Yes?'

'I know I said you could do what you want but there's a limit to how much of this I can take.'

That went for her as well. She was so close to the edge, one more rub and she'd have been flying apart around him. But she wanted to come with him inside her again and she wanted it desperately, so she put her hands on his shoulders and pushed herself up. She lifted her hips, her pulse thundering, took him in her hand and angled him so that he was poised at her entrance. Then she lowered herself onto him, slowly, feeling every inch of him, hearing his low groan and shivering when he put his hands on her waist.

'I think I might start moving,' she said hoarsely.

'Don't let me stop you.'

Nothing could stop her. She was being driven by a force that she still didn't fully understand but was all up for going with. She rolled her hips experimentally and Theo moaned, so she did it again a bit harder and this time she moaned. He felt so good. He seemed to be touching her everywhere.

She leaned forwards to kiss him and gasped as the shift in angle meant he hit a spot deep within her and set off a whole new set of explosions. She felt his hands move to her hips, guiding her, moving her, while her breasts rubbed against his hair-roughened chest, the friction rocking her world.

As the delicious pressure inside her grew and everything began to tighten she found herself moving with increasing urgency and less coordination. Her control was history. The desire and need pounding through her was relentless. Unable to help herself, she whimpered against his mouth, she might even have begged. She didn't know. All she knew was that Theo suddenly tilted his hips up and buried himself deep as she ground down, and that was it. White-hot pleasure burst inside her like a firework and lights flashed behind her eyelids and her entire world turned upside down.

Explosive. That was what that had been, thought Theo with the one brain cell capable of functioning. He'd never experienced anything like it. He'd never ceded control in bed. He'd never even considered it. But perhaps that had been a mistake because he'd just done exactly that and his mind had been blown.

The lack of self-consciousness with which Kate had explored him and the abandoned confidence with which she'd taken what she wanted was breathtaking. *She* was breathtaking. She was also lying naked beside him, uncovered and unashamed, stretching and practically purring with satisfaction, and incredibly he wanted her again.

But giving up control once was more than enough and her allure wasn't that irresistible. To prove it he would make himself wait. He would use conversation as a distraction. He might even try and get the answer to a question that had been bugging him for weeks.

Rolling onto his side, Theo propped himself up on one elbow. 'So what exactly is this?' he asked, trailing the fingers of his other hand over the tattoo at Kate's hip and feeling her shiver beneath his touch.

'It's an upside-down swallow,' she said with a breathlessness that made him briefly wonder why he'd thought it a good idea to wait.

'Why an upside-down swallow?'

'It represents me flipping the bird at the entire male sex. I was twenty and fed up with still not being able to get a date. I wanted to make a point.'

'It's pretty.'

'It's actually pretty pointless.'

'Why?'

'Because looking down on it from up here, it's the right way up, which does rather defeat the object of the exercise. I didn't think of that when I was all fired up and pissed off.'

Unexpectedly, Theo felt a faint smile curve his mouth. 'No, well, who would?'

'Ideally the tattoo artist would have had an inkling,' she said dryly. 'He supposedly had twenty years' experience. But it's fine. I'm used to it. And now it seems rather irrelevant anyway.'

His smile faded and a ribbon of concern wound through him because he hoped she wasn't referring to them. They weren't dating and they never would. This was a one, maybe two, night thing at most. Which was all it ever could be. And that was fine. The thing stabbing away at him wasn't regret. It was guilt. Because now he came to think about it he'd been remiss earlier and it had been playing on his mind.

'You looked spectacular this evening,' he said, remembering how speechless he'd been when he'd turned and seen her standing there on the balcony.

'Did I?'

'Yes.'

'Thank you. I wasn't sure.'

'The mirror doesn't lie.'

'I wouldn't know.'

'Why not?'

'I don't much like looking at myself in a mirror,' she said, frowning and biting on her lower lip, which gave him all kinds of ideas he intended to put into action later. 'Not a full-length one anyway. There's just so much of me. I went to a hall of mirrors once at a funfair when I was six and was traumatised for weeks.'

'Yet you're now wearing heels.'

'I know,' she said, flashing him a quick grin that did something strange to his chest. 'For the first time in years. Isn't that great?'

Was it? He wasn't so sure. While he was gratified by the improvement in her self-esteem and confidence, he didn't like to think what she might see if she looked him straight in the eye. He liked even less the memory of how as they'd walked to the party, their strides in synch, it had briefly, unacceptably, occurred to him that they somehow matched.

'So come on,' she said, rolling onto her side so that she faced him and fixing him with exactly the sort of disconcertingly probing look he feared. 'Your turn.'

'About what?'

'Tell me something about you that no one else knows.'

He tensed and frowned. 'I've already told you something no one else knows.' Many things, actually.

'Something else.'

'My childhood wasn't enough?'

'It doesn't have to be a big thing. It could be tiny. Humour me.' She shot him a wicked smile and for a second he marvelled at how quickly she'd gone from virgin to temptress. 'I'll make it worth your while.'

'All right,' he said, his body hardening all over again at the mere thought of just how she might go about doing that. 'I get headaches when I'm stressed. I didn't learn to read until I was sixteen. And I have a mild allergy to celery, which makes my tongue go numb.'

'There,' she said, her eyes shimmering with emotions he didn't want to even try and identify. 'You see? That wasn't so bad, was it?'

'Depends on what I want to do with my tongue.'

'And what *do* you want to do with your tongue?'

'Why don't you lie back and let me show you?'

Kate was in the kitchen making coffee on Sunday morning when there was a knock on the door of the villa.

How she'd made it downstairs in the first place she had no idea. Her entire body felt like jelly. Muscles she never knew she had ached. By rights, she ought to be exhausted. She'd only had a couple of hours' sleep. But instead she felt fabulous, on top of the world, exhilarated. Every sense was heightened. Colours were bright. Smells were intense.

Last night had been incredible. And not just from a physical point of view. When she and Theo had been able to take no more, they'd talked. Well, she had at least. His questions about her life—her upbringing, her job, that second-base bet—had been endless, his interest had been genuine, and she'd basked in the attention. She hadn't managed to get much out of him, apart from a few details about his journey to global domination, but that was okay. She had all day.

Because he was taking her to Florence. More specifically, to the Garden of Archimedes, which apparently was a museum of mathematics. He'd informed her of the plan an hour ago, when she'd suggested spending the entire day in bed, and when she'd heard it and realised that he'd remembered that numbers were her thing, her silly soft heart had melted. The plane was on standby, the finest restaurant in Florence was booked for a late leisurely lunch and she couldn't wait.

Whoever was outside knocked on the door again and Kate jumped. Abandoning the coffee pot and the lovely hot memories of last night, she walked to the door on legs that still felt a bit shaky and opened it.

On the doorstep, to her surprise, stood Daniel Bridgeman.

'*Buongiorno,*' she said, with the wide grin that she just couldn't seem to contain.

'Good morning,' he replied with an answering smile. 'May I come in?'

'Theo's in the shower.'

'No problem,' he said. 'It was you I wanted to speak to anyway.'

Oh? Why?

Kate felt her smile falter for a second and nerves fluttered in her stomach, but she held the door open for him and let him in because what else could she do?

'Would you like some coffee?' she asked, feeling a bit awkward about offering her host his own coffee as she watched him glance around the space as if for some reason checking it out.

Having apparently finished his perusal, he turned to her and shook his head. 'No, thank you.'

'The party last night was wonderful.'

'I'm delighted you enjoyed it.'

'We did.'

'I noticed. Watching you and Theo on the dance floor was revelatory.'

There was a twinkle in his eye and Kate found herself suddenly blushing. 'Yes, well, the music was good.'

'My wife has eclectic tastes.' He looked at her for a moment, his gaze suddenly shrewd, and

Kate found that for some reason she was suddenly fighting the urge to squirm. 'Do you know why I invited you and Theo here this weekend, Kate?'

'To discuss the deal?'

'Partly,' he agreed with a nod. 'I wanted to meet you. And see the two of you together.'

'Oh?'

He shook his head and smiled. 'I may be old, but I am far from stupid.'

Her pulse skipped a beat in alarm. 'No, no,' she said, thinking that now would be a really good time for Theo to put in an appearance. 'Quite right.'

'How much do you know about the history of this deal?'

'Some,' she hedged cautiously.

'I had some doubts about Theo.'

'He said.'

Daniel's grey bushy eyebrows lifted. 'Did he?'

'Yes.' She smiled at the memory. 'He was very put out by it.'

'I've spent fifty years building up my business. I'm not going to sell it to just anyone.'

'No. Of course not.'

'One thing that did concern me was your engagement.'

Oh, dear. 'In what way?' she said lightly.

'A suspicious man might question the speed and timing of it.'

'And are you suspicious?'

'On occasion.'

Dammit, what was he trying to say? 'I can understand that.'

'It's a deal that's of huge benefit to both parties. There's a lot at stake. Theo isn't a man to give up easily.'

No, he wasn't. She had first-hand experience of that, although somehow it no longer seemed to bother her. 'He won't let you down.'

'So tell me why I should sell to him.'

What? 'Me?' Kate said, her eyebrows shooting up.

'You.'

'God, I don't know,' she said. 'I actually know very little about the ins and outs of it.'

'But you know him, I assume.'

Did she? She thought she did. A bit. Maybe more than a bit now. Enough to convince Daniel Bridgeman that he had no reason to doubt Theo's integrity, at any rate. 'You're right, I do,' she said, thankfully sounding more certain than she felt. 'And I can promise you won't regret it if you do decide to sell to him. Theo can come across as ruthless, I admit, but he is honourable. He's also incredibly loyal, protective and thoughtful.' Not to mention devastatingly handsome and unbelievable in bed, although she didn't think Mr Bridgeman would appreciate that level of detail. 'You have no idea how hard he's had to work to get where he is,' she said instead. 'He didn't have the advantage of a stellar education or buckets of money to support him. He's grafted his entire adult life and continues to do so.'

'I see,' said the older man, but she hadn't finished.

'And he's an excellent listener,' she said. 'When we met I had a few self-esteem issues but he's given me the confidence to get over them and believe in myself, and that is something I will always be grateful for.'

'Interesting.'

She blushed, suddenly aware that she might have gone a bit far in her defence of him, even if everything she'd said was true. 'Yes, well, he's a decent man.'

'You make a good team,' said Daniel.

'Er…right, yes, absolutely we do.'

'As I told him over drinks on Friday night, with a fiancée like you and a baby on the way, he's a lucky man.'

Oh, dear God. The suggestion must have conjured up his worst nightmare. No wonder he'd been so broodingly distracted at dinner. 'He certainly is,' she said.

Daniel headed towards the door. 'Thank you for sparing me some of your time, Kate, and I hope to see you again soon.'

And even though she and Theo didn't make a good team and she wouldn't be seeing Daniel Bridgeman again, Kate nevertheless fixed a bright smile to her face and said, 'I hope so, too.'

Upstairs in the bathroom, Theo gripped the edge of the basin, his head swimming and his heart thundering while a cold sweat broke out all over his skin despite the icy shower he'd forced himself to take.

He hadn't meant to eavesdrop. When he'd heard Daniel and Kate talking downstairs he'd fully intended to join them, especially when Daniel had revealed his suspicions about the engagement. But then Kate had begun extolling his non-existent virtues and he'd frozen, his body filling with dread and denial and who knew what else. The passion in her voice… The sincerity… It had made his stomach churn and bile rise up his throat, and he just couldn't swallow it down.

In no way did he and Kate make a good team. They didn't make any kind of team. They would never match. And he'd been wrong when he'd told her there was nothing she could do he wouldn't like. He hadn't liked what she'd said. He didn't want anyone singing his praises. He didn't need anyone on his side. Ever.

One night of spectacular sex. That was all they'd had. He'd assumed she'd been on the same page, but it hadn't sounded as if she was. It had sounded as if she'd become...*involved*. And if he was being brutally honest she wasn't the only one.

When he thought of the uncharacteristic things he'd said and done since meeting her he realised that at some point he'd lost the sense of who he was. Despite blithely assuming he had everything under control, right from the beginning he'd allowed her to get under his skin and invade his thoughts.

Take the way he'd insisted on fixing her issues, issues that theoretically had nothing to do with him, out of some misguided non-existent sense of responsibility. Look at what he'd done with the thank-you note she'd sent him. He'd had no reason to keep it and he should have shredded it. Nevertheless he'd tucked it away in the top drawer of his desk in the office. Why? Who knew?

Then there was the red convertible parked up outside. It hadn't been the only car left. He'd had ample choice. But when he'd been presented with the options he'd recalled the wistful longing in her voice when she'd told him all those weeks ago that she'd always wanted one and he'd simply thought she'd like it. In much the same way he'd thought she might enjoy a visit to the maths museum in Florence.

And then there were the tiny snippets about himself that she'd asked for and he'd given her. She'd only wanted one. He'd given her three. Too many. Too much.

He should never have done any of it, he thought grimly as he pushed himself upright and rubbed his hands over his face. He most definitely shouldn't have slept with her again. However great the pressure of the weekend, however powerful his desire for her, he should have had better control. He'd been careless, weak and self-indulgent and that sense of imminent implosion was expanding with every second. If he didn't want everything he'd striven for to crash and burn, he had to put an end to whatever was or wasn't going on with Kate. Right now.

Shutting down and filling with steely resolve, Theo headed downstairs, and, on seeing that Daniel had gone, after muttering to Kate that he had something to take care of but wouldn't be long, left. And when he returned an hour later, the chaos churning around inside him had been dispelled. Cool, steady calm had returned and nothing, *nothing*, was going to threaten it again.

'Hi,' said Kate, greeting him with a brightness and enthusiasm that bounced straight off his armour and a kiss on the mouth that he didn't even feel. 'Are we off? Did you know that the museum has a section dedicated to Pythagoras? It focuses on puzzles inspired by his theorem and I can't *wait*.'

Too bad. 'Pack up your things.'

'Oh?' she said, staring at him in surprise. 'Why?'

'We're going home.'

Her grin faded and disappointment spread across her lovely face, and it bothered him not one jot. 'But the deal?'

'Signed.'

'So Florence?'

'Cancelled.'

'And…us?'

'Over.'

CHAPTER THIRTEEN

THROUGHOUT THE ENTIRE tautly silent journey back to a grey and wet London, Kate was accompanied by a level of disappointment that she didn't understand. The weekend might have ended abruptly and a day ahead of schedule, but she'd always known that once Theo's deal was signed that would be that. She'd always been more than all right with it, so what was this crushing sense of anticlimax all about? Why did she feel so stunned and so, well, *sad*?

None of it made any sense. Yes, she'd been excited about going to the Garden of Archimedes, but she could easily go on her own another time. She didn't need Theo to make her arrangements for her. And while another night of incredible sex would have been wonderful, it wasn't as if she wouldn't survive without it. In fact, she ought to be glad this ridiculous charade was over and she could get on with the rest of her life, starting with the visit to her sister that she had been prepared to miss.

Yet she wasn't.

Maybe it was the unexpectedness of it that was troubling her. Or the sudden inexplicable change in his mood this morning, which she still couldn't fathom. When she'd left him in the shower, he'd been thoroughly relaxed. She'd made sure of it. Yet, mere moments after the chat she and Daniel had had, he'd stormed off and returned in a very different frame of mind.

What could possibly have happened in the meantime? Had he heard what she'd had to say about him? Since she hadn't exactly been whispering he might well have done, but even if he had, why would that make him react so negatively? She'd only had positive things to say, and she was pretty sure that the false picture she'd painted of their relationship was what had got the deal signed. So really, he ought to be *thanking* her, not blanking her.

She didn't understand it, but when she asked what was wrong all she got in response were grunts and monosyllables, and that hurt because she deserved more. She *wanted* more. She wanted to know what he was thinking and what he was feeling. She wanted to burrow beneath his surface, find out what was going on and fix it. And not just because she found him insanely attractive. She also liked and admired him and cared about him. He was everything she'd told Daniel Bridgeman he was, and so much more. He was complicated and difficult and layered and fascinating. Challenging and annoying and brilliant.

And about to drop her home and drive off out of her life for good.

This really was it, Kate thought, her heart squeezing painfully at the realisation. The fake relationship that somehow no longer felt fake was actually over. Once she got out of the car she'd never see or hear from him again. Why did that hurt so much? Why did she feel as though she were being sliced in two? Was she actually going to be physically sick?

With fingers that were oddly trembling she lowered her window and turned her face towards it. The cool fresh breeze instantly calmed her churning stomach but it did nothing to alleviate the misery now scything through her body. Why had it had to end now? Why couldn't she have had one more day and one more night? Why couldn't she have had for ever?

At that, Kate instantly froze. Time seemed to skid to a halt. Her head emptied of everything but that last bewildering thought.

For ever?

What?

Why would she want that?

Why would she even *think* that?

Theo wasn't for ever.

But she was.

And, oh, dear Lord, she'd fallen in love with him.

As the truth of it landed like a blow to the chest, Kate reeled, her heart pounding, her skin tight and damp. She loved everything about him. He wasn't ruthless; he was dynamic. He wasn't lacking in empathy; he was understandably guarded. He was everything she'd ever dreamed of, plus he was sexy as hell and the father of her child and he'd been planning to take her to a maths museum.

All those feelings that she'd tried to prevent and then deny… The thrill whenever he called… The exhilaration when she was with him… The sympathy and the fury, and the leap of her heart whenever she looked at the ring… They all suddenly made sense. But how had it happened? And when? Only a week ago she'd hated him. What had changed that? Or had she never really hated him in the first place?

The questions spun around her head, tangling

with the realisation that she was crazy about him, making her heart thump with hope and bewilderment.

And despair.

Because she couldn't possibly tell him. Love had never been part of the deal. She'd merely be setting herself up for brutal rejection and abject misery. He'd be appalled.

Or would he?

What if his feelings had changed, too? What if the chilly distance he'd put between them emanated from a similar epiphany? What if he too was battling feelings he wasn't sure would be reciprocated?

No. She would not think like that. She mustn't. When it came to speculation about what Theo might or might not be thinking she was always wrong. Besides, he didn't do uncertainty.

And, actually, with regards to one particular aspect of their relationship, neither did she. Because while she still needed time to process how she felt about him and figure out what she was going to do about it, if anything, suddenly she was damned if she was going to let him drop her off and drive away without at least having *tried* to persuade him to change his mind about his involvement with their child. She wasn't going to go back to the Kate of before, afraid and in hiding. She was going to fight.

'So, Theo?' she said, nerves nevertheless tangling in her stomach as he turned a corner and her building hove into view, an indication that time was running out.

His brows snapped together. 'Yes?'

'I was wondering… What are you going to do once the deal's gone through?'

'What do you mean?' he said, shooting her a stony glance that would have had her backing right off had she not strengthened her resolve.

'Well, once you've achieved global domination, what's left?'

'Nothing,' he said. 'I'll be done.'

'Will you?'

'Yes.'

'Are you sure about that?'

'Quite sure.'

She took a deep breath and mentally crossed her fingers. 'Because if you do need another project, there's one cooking away right here.' She indicated her abdomen and watched as his gaze flickered across and down, his jaw tightening in that familiar way.

'That won't be necessary.'

'Why not?'

'You know why not.'

'No. I don't. Not really.'

'Kate.'

'History doesn't have to repeat itself,' she persisted, ignoring the warning note she could hear in his voice because she was in love with him and she had to make him see she was right.

'As I told you before, it's a risk I'm not willing to take.'

'There is no risk.'

'However much I might wish otherwise, you are both better off—and safer—without me.'

At his choice of words, hope flared inside her, spreading through her like wildfire, dizzying her with its intensity. Could it be that he *did* want them but was simply so blinded by fear he believed he didn't deserve them? Could she convince him otherwise? 'You are not your father,' she said, her throat tight and her pulse racing.

'Leave it.'

'No. It's too important.'

'I don't want to talk about it.'

Too bad. He wasn't shutting her down again. Not now. And she'd chosen her battlefield wisely. There was no escape from a moving car. 'But you should,' she said heatedly. 'You need to. You need to see what I see: a man who would go to the ends of the earth to protect and defend those that matter to him. That man would never be a danger to anyone. That man would *never* hit anyone.'

He pulled over suddenly and parked, and then turned to her, his eyes bleak, his face rigid. 'But I did, Kate,' he said bluntly. 'I did.'

She blanched, the words hovering between them, the rain hammering down on the roof of the car. 'What do you mean?'

'Exactly that.'

No. He wouldn't. He couldn't. 'When? Who?'

'My mother. I was sixteen.'

She recoiled with shock, but right down to her marrow she knew that it couldn't be that simple. 'What happened?'

'Nothing happened.'

'I don't believe you. There has to be some explanation.'

'There isn't.'

'Circumstances, then?' she said, because she was not going to let this go and she refused to believe it of him. 'Tell me the circumstances.'

'The day I'd planned to leave,' he said, his voice flat and emotionless in a way that intensified the ache in her chest, 'I told her to grab what she needed. She said no. I begged. My father came home, off his head as usual. She told him what I'd asked her to do and he flew into a rage. He punched me in the stomach and I'd had enough. For the first time in my life I retaliated. My mother went to protect him and my fist caught her on the cheek. She told me to get out. So I did.'

He spoke matter-of-factly, but she could hear the trace of emotion behind what he said, the guilt, betrayal, the rejection, the abandonment. 'It was an accident,' she said, her words catching on the lump in her throat.

'Was it?'

'Yes.'

'That's who I really am, Kate.'

'It isn't. It really isn't.' She took a deep breath and stepped into the terrifying unknown. 'I've fallen in love with you, Theo. I don't know when or how, but I love you and trust you with every cell of my being.'

He barely moved a muscle in response. 'Then you've made a mistake,' he said flatly. 'I can never be the man you want me to be.'

For a moment her heart shattered, pain pummelling through her at the realisation he was adamant in his belief, but then, quite suddenly, anger flared deep inside her, rushing along her veins and setting fire to her nerve-endings. How dared he tell her she'd made a mistake? How dared he dismiss her feelings? And how dared he continue to reject their child?

'You already are the man I want you to be,' she said fiercely. 'Everything I told Daniel was true. But you are also a coward.'

His eyebrows shot up at that, a chink in the icy facade at last. 'What?'

'You heard,' she said, burning up with frustration and hurt. 'You're a coward. History *doesn't* have to repeat itself. There are choices you can make. There are choices you've *already* made. You are not just your father's son. You're also your mother's. And when it comes to *our* child, you're only half the equation. I have never felt in danger with you, Theo, even when I pushed you and pushed you and you hated it. In fact, I've never felt safer or better protected.'

She stopped, breathing hard, but he didn't say anything. His fingers flexed on the steering wheel, his knuckles white and his face tight, but his simmering anger was nothing compared to hers.

'I think you're scared,' she said hotly. 'I think you're scared of rejection and abandonment and that's why you're not prepared to take a risk on us. And you know what? I get it. I'm scared, too. This pregnancy terrifies me. Everyone I love has a habit of leaving me one way or another. My brother, my father, even my sister. Right now, I miss my mother more than I ever thought possible and it hurts so very much. And then there's the guilt. My God, the guilt. Every time I see Milly, the fact that she will never get the chance to fall in love, have a family, crucifies me.' She shook her head. 'So I don't have a clue what I'm going to do and I'm petrified my anxieties will take over, but I no longer have the luxury of wallowing in my hang-ups. Of being selfish. I have a child to think about. You could, too. And you could have me. Because Daniel was right. We do make a good team. We could make a great one. We could be a family. The one that I want and the one that I know, deep down, you want. And don't you dare give me that "I'm better off alone" rubbish. No one is. Everyone needs someone.'

'I don't.'

'You *do*. Don't you *want* to be happy?' she asked, hearing the faint desperation in her voice but not caring. 'Don't you *want* to let go of the past and look to the future?'

Silence fell and stretched and for the briefest of moments she thought she'd got through to him and hope leapt, but when he spoke it was with an icy calm that splintered her heart and shattered her dreams. 'Why is it so hard to understand, Kate?' he said coldly. 'I don't need happiness and I don't want you.'

'But—'

'What I do want, however, is for you to get out of my car. Now.'

Shaking all over and in agony, Kate closed the door to her flat behind her and sank to the floor, her heart shattering as the sobs she'd held at bay while scrabbling to get out of Theo's car now racked her body.

His brutal rejection of everything she'd offered him was crucifying. Not only had she laid the possibility of a happy future, a happy life on a platter for him, she'd revealed her fears and handed him her heart. And he'd trampled all over it.

Tears streamed down her face and she curled up on the floor, exhaustion and despair descending like a heavy black cloud. She'd given it her best shot and she'd failed. If only she hadn't barged in there with her declaration of love. If only she'd stuck with the plan to keep it to herself for a while. If only she hadn't fallen in love with him in the first place.

She'd been such an idiot. She'd recognised the risk to her heart he presented and she'd blithely assumed she'd be able to handle it. Why she'd ever thought that when she had zero experience in such matters and the physical and emotional attraction she felt for him was so strong she had no idea. But it was too late for regret because now here she was at the bottom of that slippery slope, and it was just as wretched and miserable as she'd imagined.

Why couldn't he have been willing to give them a chance? Why couldn't he have let her help him? Love him? She had so much to give. What if he just needed time? What if she gave him some space and then tried again?

But no, she told herself with a watery sniff as she angrily brushed away the tears that continued to leak out of the corners of her eyes. She'd be banging her head against a brick wall. She had to stop hoping and imagining and wishing. Theo wasn't going to suddenly and miraculously wake up one morning realising he was in love with her and deciding he *did* want them. He was too damaged. Too entrenched in his beliefs. He was determined to remain alone, an island barricaded from the soaring highs and wretched lows of life.

And however much that hurt, and, oh, how it did, she had to accept it, get up and move on.

CHAPTER FOURTEEN

IN THE DAYS that followed their return to London, Theo was convinced he'd done one hundred per cent the right thing by letting Kate go. He would not tarnish her with his darkness. His actions—and his inaction—brought about the destruction of other people and he would not destroy her, too. Or their child. He didn't deserve happiness and he had no right to take what she had offered. Despite what she believed, he wasn't, and could never be, the man she wanted him to be. And when he thought of the way she'd gone on the attack, which was all the damn time since he couldn't seem to get it out of his head, he was absolutely certain that there was nothing he would have done differently.

He knew he was no coward. She had no idea how much strength and courage it took to stand alone and apart and not seize what deep down he'd always tried to deny he craved. And he was not wallowing or selfish, despite what she might have implied. His concerns were current and real.

So as he'd watched her stumble up the steps to her building he'd told himself that she and her baby would be fine now. He'd driven home and poured himself one drink and then another and then another. The next day he'd gone into the office and thrown himself into work. The deal had been signed. The details were being hammered out. Everything was proceeding smoothly.

But now, two hellish weeks later, he found himself wondering, where was the peace? Where was the sense of achievement? Why was he still so frustratingly restless? And why couldn't he stop pacing?

The sense of impending doom he'd assumed would vanish once he'd dealt with Kate hadn't. Instead, it was larger and darker and more oppressive than ever. And as for order and control that he'd expected to return, he currently felt as if he were hanging on a cliff face by his fingertips. He was popping painkillers like candy and he was snapping at anyone who had the misfortune to cross his path.

What was the matter with him? Why couldn't he concentrate? Why couldn't he eat or sleep? And why hadn't he returned the ring to the jewellers? Kate had returned it to him by courier the day after they'd arrived back. The sight of it had cleaved him in two, but he'd kept it on his desk where it sparkled away at him all sodding day and he had no idea why.

Nor could he work out why he hadn't announced that he and Kate had decided to go their separate ways. The deal was sealed. The contract could not now be broken. A quick press release to announce that their engagement was off would be the easiest thing to do. So why did it feel like the hardest? Why was he still putting it off?

It was all as confusing as hell, but not nearly as confusing as the doubts that had started bothering him a couple of days ago and were now sprouting up all over the place. What if she was right and he was wrong? was the main one, the one that tortured his every waking moment. The minute he crushed it in one place, up it popped somewhere else, churning up his insides and driving him demented.

It couldn't go on.

He couldn't go on.

Not any more.

As the strength suddenly left his body, Theo sank into the sofa, his elbows on his knees, and buried his head in his hands.

He was so damn sick of it. Sick of the torment and the fighting and the bone-crushing loneliness. All his life he'd been alone. He had no siblings and he'd allowed no one to get close. Not even Kate, who'd made him doubt and fear and hope. Who'd pushed her way through his defences and stabbed at where he was weakest and who he might as well admit he adored.

He couldn't do denial any longer. His impenetrability was shot. As the walls around his heart crumbled, pain and regret sliced through him. She'd offered him everything he'd ever wanted and he'd thrown it back in her face. And why? Because she'd been right—he *had* been scared. He'd always been scared.

But, really, what was there to be afraid of? Hadn't he demonstrated time and time again that he had broken the mould? How many times had he been pushed yet stayed in control? He wasn't his father. He never had been. Never would be. Deep down he knew that. So what if that wasn't the real issue? What if he *did* fear rejection and abandonment?

He'd never forget the pain and the guilt, the distress and the trepidation that had gripped every inch of him when he'd shut the door on the flat he'd called home and what little family he'd had. He'd had money and a plan, but that first night he'd spent alone in a cheap nearby hotel had been so cold, so bleak, and the only way he'd been able to move forward was to accept the icy emptiness, adopt it and turn it into armour.

The actions of his mother had cut deep, but it had been fourteen years since she'd looked at him with accusation and disgust. There'd been nothing he could do to save her. He'd given her every opportunity to escape and she'd made her choice and it hadn't been him. There'd been nothing he could have done to save Mike either. Deep down he knew that because he'd done the research and asked the questions.

So he had to forgive himself and let it all go. Because how long was he going to deny himself the future he'd always dreamed of? How long was he going to be able to carry on knowing Kate was out there on her own because of his own blind stupidity?

God, he loved her. She was brave and forthright and confronted whatever life threw at her with her chin up and challenge in her eyes. He wanted her and he wanted their child. And he'd rejected them both.

When he thought of what he'd said to her, and

the way he'd said it, he felt sick to his stomach. The ice, the disdain, the cruelty. He could recall every single word and they sliced at him like knives. What the hell had he done? he wondered, shame slamming into him as he broke into a cold sweat. And what the hell could he do to fix it?

The last fortnight for Kate had been something of a roller coaster. One minute she was doing fine, concentrating on putting one foot in front of the other as she got through the days, the next she was dissolving into tears, heartbroken and wishing for what could never be.

A week ago she'd gone to a doctor's appointment and when she'd heard the fluttering whoosh of her baby's heartbeat she'd completely lost it. When she'd visited Milly, who'd grilled her excitedly about the trip to Italy and bombarded her with questions about the non-existent wedding, she'd had to leave before she broke down. Swinging between intense despair and desperate hope that the fact that Theo hadn't issued an announcement about their separation might mean something, she was mostly a wreck and she'd lost count of how many tubs of ice cream she'd consumed.

But while acceptance that he wasn't going to

change his mind still shredded her heart it *was* getting easier. Her appetite had returned and she'd stopped waking up in the middle of the night in tears. And look at the way she could now go without thinking about him for a whole five minutes. See how the urge to call him and beg him to give them a chance was gradually diminishing. That was huge progress.

And that wasn't the only area in which she was moving on. The day before yesterday, she'd grabbed a large plastic bag and filled it with the ill-fitting clothes she'd once bought because they made her feel dainty. Then she'd ordered a full-length mirror, which had arrived this morning. If she was going to carry on walking around in her underwear, which she'd taken to doing since everything else was getting tight, she figured she might as well see what she looked like doing it. So what if she was going to become the size of a whale and probably just as cumbersome? Her body was building a baby. It wasn't anything to be ashamed of. It was magnificent. And who cared if she didn't fit in? What was so great about being the same as everyone else anyway?

Besides, she wanted to be able to admire her fabulous new haircut properly. She'd wanted short hair for as long as she could remember but she'd always worried that it would make her look even bigger. And it probably did, but she didn't care, she loved it anyway. Statuesque was how she was going to think of herself from now on. Fearless. And strong.

Because she was all that and more. She'd been wrong about Theo being responsible for the changes she'd undergone. It had been her. All her. She didn't need him. She didn't need anyone. And when she was ready she'd find another man with whom she could wear heels and walk in synch. In Holland, perhaps. Dutch men were the tallest on the planet. They had an average height of one hundred and eighty-two point five centimetres. She knew. She'd looked it up.

In the meantime she had plenty to occupy herself. She had work to find. She had Milly and the baby to focus on. That was more than enough. She didn't need Theo. She didn't need anyone. She was more than capable of doing this on her own. She'd be fine. In fact, she *was* fine.

The buzzer sounded, making her jump and jolting her out of her thoughts. She put down the knife with which she was chopping onions for soup for supper and wiped her streaming eyes. Padding into the hall, she picked up the handset. 'Yes?' she said with a sniff.

'It's Theo.'

At the sound of his voice, the voice that had tormented her dreams and which she'd never ever forget, Kate nearly dropped the handset. Her heart skipped a beat and then began to thunder, the surge of love, need and hope colliding with doubt and wariness. Why was he here? What did he want? And what was she going to do?

The part of her that was still crushed by the way he'd rejected her was tempted to tell him to get lost. Yet him on her doorstep was precisely what she'd been dreaming of, and so even though she was so vulnerable where this man was concerned, even though he had the power to destroy her so completely she might never recover if she wasn't extremely careful, she knew she was no more going to hang up on him than she was going to be a petite size six.

'Come up.'

That was one hurdle cleared, thought Theo grimly, his gut churning with rare nerves as the door buzzed and he pushed his way in. Now for the rest.

As he took to the stairs, it occurred to him that for the first time in decades he had no plan. He had no idea what he was going to say. Once he'd realised how much of a fool he'd been, all he'd focused on was getting here. The only thing he *did* know was that he'd come to fight for the woman he loved and to get her back, whatever it took, whatever the cost, and he wasn't leaving until he'd achieved it.

His throat dry and his pulse racing, he banged on her door and a second later it swung open and there she was, standing there in a dressing gown, her eyes red and shimmering with unshed tears.

'Are you all right?' he asked gruffly, the idea that he could have done that to her, *had* done that to her stabbing him like a dagger in the chest.

'I'm fine,' she replied with a sniff.

Another thought entered his head then, a thought that chilled his blood and for a moment stopped his heart. 'The baby?'

'It's fine, too.'

'Then why are you crying?' he demanded, the indescribable relief flooding through him sharpening his tone.

She blew her nose and gave a shrug. 'Onions.'

He went still. 'What?'

'I've been chopping onions.'

Right. So. Her tears weren't because of him. They were because of onions. That was good. Wasn't it? 'In a dressing gown?'

She lifted her chin a fraction and arched an eyebrow, and he felt a great thud of lust and love slam through him. 'In my underwear, if you must know.'

He'd rather not. The images immediately flashing through his head were immensely distracting and did unsettling things to his equilibrium. Nevertheless, as much as he'd like to pull her into his arms, undo the belt and see exactly what she had on beneath, he kept his eyes up and his hands in his pockets. 'You've had your hair cut.'

'Yes.'

'It suits you.'

'I know,' she said. 'I've also bought a full-length mirror and am considering a move to Holland.'

The ground beneath his feet shifted. What the hell? 'Holland?'

She nodded briefly. 'Holland.'

'Why?'

'Why not?'

He knew of a dozen reasons why not. 'I thought you didn't travel much.'

She shrugged. 'Things change,' she said, and it hit him like a blow to the head that they had. She wasn't sitting at home pining for him. She was getting her hair cut and buying mirrors. She was moving on. Without him. And it was his own damn fault. He yanked his hands out of his pockets and shoved them through his hair, his heart pounding with the very real fear that he'd blown it for good. 'Don't go.'

'You don't get to tell me what to do any more, Theo.'

'I know I don't.'

'Then why are you here?'

'There are so many reasons, I barely know where to start.'

She frowned. 'Is there a problem with the deal?'

'No.'

'Then…?'

'May I come in?'

'No,' she said, folding her arms across her chest and straightening her spine magnificently. 'Whatever you have to say, you can say it out here.'

'All right,' he muttered, beginning to pace in an effort to untangle the jumbled thoughts in his head and calm the panic that he was too late, that he might have already lost her. 'First of all, I wanted to tell you that you were right.'

'About what?'

'Every single point you made in the car. Deep

down, I *have* been afraid of rejection and abandonment and it's why I've always kept people at arm's length. But the truth is I ache with loneliness. I want to be happy, Kate, and I want what you offered. You. Our child. The chance to be a family.' He took a deep breath. 'Because I love you.'

She went very still and when she spoke it was almost a whisper. 'What did you say?'

'I love you,' he said, staring at her unwaveringly, unwilling to miss even a flicker of reaction. 'And I need you. You have no idea how much. You are incredible.'

She swallowed hard. 'But you threw me away.'

'Yes,' he said, the memory of his careless brutality skewering him.

'It hurt.'

At the pain in her eyes, his chest tightened as if caught in a vice. 'I know. And I'm sorry. For all of it. For the way I spoke to you in the car. For blackmailing you in the first place. For everything.' He cleared his throat. 'The thing is, Kate, for so long I've believed the world is a safer place if I'm alone and that detachment and distance was the only way to achieve that. It always has been.'

He paused and rubbed his hands over his face

as he forced himself to continue. 'My earliest memory is of my father hitting my mother in the face. I can still see her on the floor, him looming over her, huge and angry while she curled up tight. We were terrified every time he came home. I used to wake up to the sounds of crying and shattering glass. I had nightmares. From the youngest age I wanted to protect her, but I couldn't and the sense of failure and hopelessness was all-consuming. I learned to shut down and switch off, and it became so natural I was barely aware I was doing it, or continued to do it. And, yes, I got out, but not before picking up a lot of other damaging belief, especially the "my way or the highway" approach to doing things, which could be attributed to my success or it could just as well be learned. And that's another thing. Success is an easy place to hide, and if no one ever challenges you it becomes even easier.'

He looked at her, willing her to understand and to forgive. 'But you did challenge me, Kate. You *do* challenge me. At first I tried to resist, tried to control it, but that was always going to be a battle I was going to lose. And I have lost it. Which is fine, because I don't want to hide behind my hang-ups any more. I want to de-programme and learn to live my life with you and our child. You have no idea how badly I want to meet him or her. I can't stop thinking about who they'll look like. I want to be the kind of father I never had. But most of all I want you on my side. By my side. I want everything you have to give and to give you everything you want in return because you deserve to have it.'

He stopped and focused on her, but he couldn't tell what she was thinking and he went cold, his pulse thudding in his ears and dread whipping through him. 'But maybe I'm not what you want any more,' he said, his throat suddenly tight and his voice cracking. 'Maybe I'm too late. Am I?'

All Kate could do was shake her head. The lump the size of Ireland that was lodged in her throat was preventing her from speaking, and her heart was so full she could barely think. Theo loved her. He wanted her. He'd opened up to her, trusting her with his greatest fears and his deepest vulnerabilities and it was everything she'd dreamed of but thought she'd never have.

'You're not too late,' she said, her voice thick with emotion, the need to dispel the uncertainty in his expression and the tension gripping his large, powerful body all-consuming.

His breath caught. His gaze sharpened. A muscle hammered in his jaw. 'No?'

'No.'

'I am still what you want?'

'Yes,' she said with a nod. 'And more. I love you.'

'Thank God for that,' he muttered, striding forward, taking her in his arms and kissing her hard until her head spun and her stomach melted. 'I really thought I'd screwed up beyond salvation.'

'What took you so long?'

'As you may have noticed, I can, on occasion, be rather single-minded.'

She leaned back in his arms and arched an eyebrow. 'On occasion?' she asked with a giddy grin.

'All right. More than on occasion. Once I embark on a course of action I'm not easily derailed. I always know what I'm doing. I always think I'm right. There's safety and security in that. But then I met you and that was shot to hell. I found myself making reckless suggestions and behaving in ways I didn't recognise and it terrified me.' He looked deep into her eyes as if still unable to believe she was there. 'And then somehow you became the plan,' he said in wonder. 'I love you, Kate, and you should know I don't intend to let you go.'

'And you should know,' she said, pressing

closer and winding her arms round his neck, 'that however tough things get, I will never walk away. I will always be on your side.'

'Will you marry me?' he asked, his eyes blazing with such love and tenderness that her own began to sting. 'For real?'

And as happiness burst through her like sunshine she tucked her head into his shoulder and sighed, 'I will.'

EPILOGUE

Two and a half years later

'SO APPARENTLY,' SAID KATE, sticking two candles into the dinosaur cake she'd spent most of the morning making, 'if you measure a child on its second birthday and double it, that's the height they're going to end up being.'

Theo glanced over from where their toddler son was ripping wrapping paper into shreds, his chest filling with emotion as it never failed to do. 'What's the verdict?'

'Five foot eight.'

His eyebrows shot up. 'Seriously?'

'No, only joking,' she said, with a blinding grin that still stole his breath. 'Six foot four, actually.'

'That's my boy.'

And in three months' time they'd have twin daughters.

Theo didn't like to think how close he'd come to throwing it all away. If Kate hadn't given him another chance... If she hadn't believed in him...

But she had and she did. Every single day. The deal had taken a year to finalise, and once it was done, his company was indeed the biggest of its kind. But it wasn't that that had given him peace. It was his family. Daniel Bridgeman had once called him a lucky man. And he was. He was the luckiest man in the world.

* * * * *